DRIVE

A Novel

ALSO BY ROB ROBERGE

More Than They Could Chew (Dark Alley/Harper Collins)
Working Backwards From The Worst Moment Of My Life (Red Hen)

DRIVE

A Novel

Rob Roberge

Hollyridge Press
Venice, California

© 2010 Rob Roberge

Hollyridge Press
P.O. Box 2872
Venice, California 90294

Cover and Book Design by Rio Symth
Cover Photo ©Toddtaulman | Dreamstime.com
Author Photo by Jeff Amaral
Manufactured in the United States of America by Lightning Source

ISBN-13: 978-0-9772298-4-0 (Hdk)
ISBN-10: 0-9772298-4-X (Hdk)
ISBN-13: 978-0-9843100-4-3 (Pbk)
ISBN-10: 0-9843100-4-5 (Pbk)

15 14 13 12 11 10   10 9 8 7 6 5 4 3 2 1

To Gayle,
who makes the world a more beautiful, complex
and wonderful place, with thanks and love for everything

There is no way one can reduce desire in order to make it emerge, emanate, from the dimension of need...
—Jacques Lacan, *Ethics*

Drive

Florida. Summer, 1994

 1

L IKE MOST EVERYONE around here in one way or another, I
work for The Chicken Man. Rube Parcell, AKA The Chicken
Man AKA Chicken AKA The Chief, depending on your relation to
him, is my boss. I don't pay much attention to money stuff, and even I
know that he's got two trucking companies, a small commercial airline,
three meat-packing plants, and a few Bally's gyms. This is all in addition to
the twenty or so fried chicken joints that gave him two of his nicknames.

You've seen him, or someone like him anyway, on late night TV.
Barking all about the best chicken in town and mesquite grills and his
mammy's recipe and tangy this and mouth-watering that. The Chicken
Man says BRING THE FAMILY, the ad screams. Over twenty loca-
tions—one near you.

A month ago, I knew as close to nothing as you can get about all
this. Then I get a call asking me to come up from Miami to Tampa for
a business meeting.

"Who?" I said to the voice on the other end.

"Rube Parcell. You've never heard of him?"

"No sir. I have not."

"Don't let him know that," the voice said.

And that was it. I had no idea what the meeting was about. I figured some painting job, and I didn't have much interest in taking a crew
all the way up to Tampa. You can't keep an eye on a crew at that distance
unless you make two trips a week to see the job site and I wasn't sure, no
matter what the money, that I needed the headache. Later the same day
of the call, though, a first class airline ticket shows up at my office, and I
figure I'll give a listen to what this Parcell has to say.

"Son, you're a legend," Parcell says to me as I enter his office.

"Thank you," I say, not knowing what the hell he's talking about.

"Ben Thompson is a down-right legend, isn't he, Earl?"

"That he is, Chief," Earl says.

"Just what we need. Local boy makes good and comes home? Or vice versa. Comes home and then makes good."

"Yes sir," Earl says. "Home cooking."

"This isn't about a paint job?" I say and look back and forth between the two thick men in front of me. Parcell looks to be in his late forties, one of those rich, tanned guys. I think he runs on his own beach. He's got the look of a gin drinker, meaty, but not fat. Thick, sausage fingers.

"Paint job?" Rube Parcell says. "Hell no. Boy, you've sold yourself short for too many god-damned years and that's going to stop. It's going to stop today. In this office."

"I don't know where you're going with this," I say. "But I'm a painter. Been one for ten years." Then it hits me where I've seen this guy before. Take away the suit, throw on some overalls and a straw hat and there it is. "You're The Chicken Man," I say.

His smile evaporates into the air and gets sucked out of the room. Both he and Earl have looks on their faces like I said I liked to fuck kids and set fire to nursing homes.

"Boy," Rube Parcell says. "I hear that phrase out of your mouth one more time and I'll rip your trachea out." He looks over at Earl, who's mixing two drinks by the bar. "Ten men have detached tracheas. How many die?"

"Nine," Earl says, bored. He doesn't look up from the drinks.

"Nine out of ten. I like to give a stupid bastard a chance. That could be you, Ben Thompson. Like those odds?"

"No, Mr. Parcell." I swallow hard, get one of those slasher-movie images—Rube Parcell is Bruce Lee, ripping at my throat and holding the bubbly mess in front of me as I drop to the ground.

"Better," he says. He sits behind his desk and looks out his window over the city. "I own a lot of things," he says. "You seem to know about the chicken franchises." He smiles. "But there's more—a hell of a lot more—to Rube Parcell than some Hee-Haw suit on TV yapping at insomniacs with the IQs of doorknobs. That ain't me, but I'll do whatever it takes to get stupid crackers to swallow my chickens."

"Understood," I say.

"Understood, hell. You understand nothing. Break that down," he says. "Nothing. No-Thing. Not a thing. Shut up and listen when you're being talked to, Ben Thompson."

Parcell stares at me, this wide grin on his face. I take my eyes off him and look at the carpet.

"You know anything about the Gulf Coast League?" he says.

"Read some," I say. Which is true. I've read a couple of articles that've been longer than they otherwise would have been in another year. The baseball strike has made the smallest, most chicken-shit sports happening—like the debut of the Gulf Coast League—news.

"How would you like to be the first coach of The Sarasota Sun?"

I look at him. "You're serious."

"I am."

"You could do better," I say.

"Don't tell Rube Parcell what he can and cannot do. My god, I do hate that. You are the choice, my choice and my choice is the choice, to coach this team. I need butts in the seats and you, Ben Thompson, local legend, will put them there."

"You know I'm not really local?" I say. "Raised in Connecticut."

"Played ball in Miami. Miami F-L-A," he says, using the old postal abbreviation. "That's enough. People love you."

"People don't know me."

He looks grim. "Now there you go, telling Rube Parcell his business. People love you, boy."

"OK," I say.

"Tell me," he says.

"Tell you?"

"Tell me people love Ben Thompson. I need to know you're right for this. Attitude-wise."

"I'm not sure I am."

He has this I'm-your-favorite-uncle thing about him. You meet Rube Parcell and—if he likes you—you feel as if this stranger actually cares if you live or die. He looks at me, a mixture of concern and pride. "Say it, son."

The air conditioner hums and clicks with steady quiet efficiency. I listen to its rhythm for a while and get taken in by it, let my mind sort of drift and look out the window. I haven't been around basketball for ten years. I'll shoot free-throws every now and again, but I've avoided it for the most part. My knee went, my love for the game went with it. Took five years before I could even watch a single game on TV. And I'm thinking: Coach? Ben Thompson? Coach Ben Thompson? An eight-week playing season? Times change. People change. And I'm thinking that maybe there's some unfinished business with me and basketball. Coach. Sure. Why not?

"I'll take it," I say.

"Say it," Rube Parcell says. "People love you."

A plane moves silently outside the window, left to right, and disappears. People love me? And I've got this scrolling list in my head that says otherwise. Name after name runs through my head. A list with ex prefixes. Ex-friends. Ex-coaches. Ex-teammates. Ex-wife.

Coach.

"People love me," I say. Parcell gives me a marine drill sergeant I-didn't-hear-you-right look.

"People love Ben Thompson," I say.

 2

PEOPLE, most of whom I never met, did, at one time, love Ben Thompson very much. The stuff The Chicken Man said about me being a legend is true. Or was true, at one point. I'm number two all-time in Florida College scoring behind Rick Barry. Look it up. Ben Thompson—behind Barry, ahead of everyone else.

 3

I WRAP UP some of the painting business with my ex-brother-in-law Claude. I tell him to take the profits on any jobs I'm not in on, and send me money from the jobs I did that we're waiting on money. Tell him I'll be back in ten weeks, maybe twelve. I empty what little I have out of my apartment and put it in the back of my Toyota, hit Alligator Alley and head north to Sarasota.

Home. Room number eleven in an apartment building owned by The Chicken Man. The apartment building is an old hotel from the fifties, a place called, then and now, The Palms. Not a living palm tree in sight. A few palm skeletons crackle in the breeze, looking like huge corn husks—all gray and brown and tired. Twenty-four rooms. Two floors. Six-over-six, separated by a pool—ten feet at the deep end—

with an old, rusted diving board that creaks and threatens to flop into the water the minute someone stands on it. What used to be the coffee shop has been turned into what looks like a tool shed—there's drop cloths, paint buckets, some tool boxes and welding equipment in the middle of the dusty floor. A nice hotel, maybe, before Interstate 75 cut its way north and south, forever reducing the tourist business on 41 to run-off. Trickle-down tourism.

Down the street, the Hob Nob cafe—good for bad coffee and abusive waitresses—and, a little further down, the Bunker, an underground bar owned by my friend, Terry Willis. Terry was the grad assistant at Miami when I was there. The proximity to The Bunker—and the fact that it's ten miles south of town—is the main reason I asked Parcell to let us stay at this place.

The Chicken Man wanted the team in the downtown Holiday Inn. I told him it was best to keep players away from fun and entertainment. Told him he'd get a better team this way. As long as the team never finds out that it's my fault that they sleep in these shitty rooms, bordered on two sides by chicken farms, I should be fine. I needed to be close to a friend, and Terry was the only friend I had on Florida's west coast.

You go to The Bunker, you park, you walk to the door and then it's down fifteen steps before you see the gray-yellow light of the bar. Sarasota's hot, over ninety and humid, in the summer—The Bunker sits about ten feet and twenty degrees beneath the heat.

4

I'M TRYING to solidify the bench rotation and there's all this noise coming from the next room. Sounds like a fight but no one's talking. No screams, no name calling. I check the room plan to make sure it's not one of mine. And it's not. I'm room eleven, the players are in one through ten.

I put the room chart down and go back to my notes. Starting five—Kenny Cash, Buddy Grant, Mike Morris, Darnell Latimore, and Jason Childs—is easy but the bench gives me trouble. Hedda's got a power forward's game in a point guard's body, which is the problem with women playing in men's leagues—even if they have the game, they're forced to play out of position. She'll have to back up Childs at point. What can I do with Steve Gates? Too slow for big guard, too small for the three spot. Plus, his wheels are dead. Lost his vertical after the second surgery and his leg has a wobble. He's shot, but he's here and—if I use him, it's got to be at shooting guard behind Cash. He can't defend anyone, anyway, so I might as well put him where he can score.

My bottom players—we've got a short ten player roster to keep costs down—are all zeros. A European import—Peter "The Great" Karpov, who is not only far from great, but he smokes cigarettes and has no endurance or real ability beyond a pretty shot; Len Shasky, a midget—5'8"—and not quick enough to make up for his size; and Stan Fillmore, who's not even a basketball player. Fillmore's a local football hero that played for the Tampa Bay Buccaneers, and wanted to give hoops a try. The Chicken Man thought he might sell a few tickets, so we took him in the tenth round. I look at these last three names on the list and—no matter how hard I try—I can't envision a game situation where I'd want any of them on the floor. Still, you need bodies for practice.

The fight next door starts again. Hard smashing against the wall. It's none of my business, but someone could get hurt. I knock on twelve's door and hear the thumps and smashes, but from the door, I hear grunts and groans I couldn't hear from my room. I knock harder and harder still the third time.

"What?"

And I can't believe what I'm seeing. Cheap apartment life is full of freaks and hookers and pimps and strange noises but this in front of me is new. It's a man—scrawny, maybe six feet, 135. His hair's blond and stringy—MTV hair. He's got a pair of cut-off Chinos on, he's barefoot and he's covered in what looks like used motor oil. Streaked and smeared all over him. Beneath the oily grime, two nipple rings gleam in the porch light.

"What?" he says again.

"The noise," I say. "I was worried."

"Noise?" he says. His eyes, they don't quite register—they've got that Manson on the cover of *Life* intensity—and I think I might be in deeper than I want to be.

"Noise," I say. "A thumping." Still nothing in his eyes. "Against the wall."

He smiles one of those you're-in-a-foreign-country smiles that says, Yes, I understand you now, strange person.

"Art," he says.

And he seems friendly enough, even if he's weird and I offer my hand. "Ben Thompson," I say. I look down at his motor oil hands and pull my hand back and wave like I'm getting the check.

"No man." He opens the door. "I'm not art, I'm Bone. The noise you heard—the noise was art."

I'm Bone? The noise was art? Where the fuck am I?

"I want your opinion," he says. "Can you come in?"

"Come in," I repeat, which is a bad habit. People have a tendency to think you're a moron. Against the far wall, the one that backs mine, is the source of the noise. Streaked against the wall are black marks, what looks like paint. It looks more like paint, anyway, on the wall, than it does on Bone.

"What do you think?" he says.

I think there's paint all over the wall. I think I'm trapped in a ho- tel room in a strange city with a crazy person. A nice crazy person, but crazy nevertheless and the nice part might only be momentary. Scissors cuts paper and crazy cuts nice.

"I think you might be in trouble," I say. Then, not wanting to of- fend him: "I mean, it's beautiful, but the landlord might have something to say about it."

"Uncle Chicken?" he says. "You got it wrong. I'm the manager here. You got a problem, you call me. You got a problem with me, there's no one to call."

"You're a Parcell?"

"Mom married a Parcell," Bone says. "There is a very large difference."

"What's that?" I say. "The difference."

"The difference is that my mother married Earl Parcell, which makes her very wealthy. She, nor I, however, are Parcells. Which means we are not insufferable assholes. Follow?"

"I think so," I say.

"So you know Uncle Chicken?"

"I call him The Chicken Man," I say. "Not to his face, though."

Bone taps his head a couple times, winks. "Loud and clear," he says. "I hear you." He walks back toward his fridge, and opens the door. "Beer?"

"No thanks," I say. "Can't"

He comes back into the living room with an Old Milwaukee, flips the top, drinks down heavy. "Old Swill," he says. "Tastes even better with paint on your tongue."

"Is that toxic?"

He shakes his head. "Nope. You're thinking oils."

Which is true. I was thinking oils. Thinking Van Gogh. Thinking black tongues and night cafes and insanity. I nod.

"So. Now that you know I won't get into trouble. What do you think?"

I look at the wall for the first time, really. Before was only a quick glance. Bone is likable, there's something nice and easy about him. The wall? It looks like what you might expect—like a six-foot naked guy covered himself in paint and ran into it. Then filled his mouth with paint and spat at it.

"It's nice," I lie, not wanting to hurt his feelings.

 5

THE GULF COAST League has a draft, but it's not anything like any draft anyone's seen on TV. The NBA draft, you've got the top twenty, twenty-five, picks all sitting in a room off to the side. You've got reporters from around the world. A kid's name gets called and he struts up on stage, gets a baseball cap with his new team's logo, his image gets beamed to a satellite out in space and lands in living rooms from Miami to Singapore. Their moms and dads clutch each other and smile. Kid after kid gets called—the first-rounders get guaranteed contracts into the millions.

The Gulf Coast League? We had tapes on a few players—Latimore's been in the NBA. Hedda Davis was two-time women's player of the year in college—with our third pick, she became the third or forth woman to be drafted into a men's league. I told The Chicken Man to stay away from her—I didn't want to turn the team into a media circus—but he's the owner and he thought she'd sell tickets. She's a player, though, and I think she's the first woman to make the cut and get a roster slot. Cash, Gates and Childs have all played minor league ball, so we knew what we had. The rest—from our sixth pick to our tenth—were just names. I asked around, read their stats and called their agents. But for the most part, The Chicken Man and I picked blind.

We call kids up on the phone and tell them they're a draft pick of the Sarasota Sun. And they say the Sarasota Who? The Sarasota What? Our first-round pick, Kenny Cash, he didn't even know about the league, let alone the team.

Kenny "Money" Cash played at Vanderbilt for two years, went to Italy and flopped in the European leagues. At practice, he wears his Vandy jersey—no way he's going to walk around in the Italian one—someone wanting to get ahead never brags about failure.

I watch him out on the court—he rains down jumper after jumper and it's a beautiful thing to see. Going right, or squared straight-up, Money's as good a shooter as there is on this planet. I watch him drop five in a row. Money's the first on the court for practice; the last to leave. He mistakes extra hours for extra work. Work is playing to your weakness. Money? He comes an hour early and shoots jumpers going right, he stays late and shoots jumpers going right. I've tried telling him: You work your weakness, that's practice—you work your strength, that's validation. But he's a kid. Never saw me play, never heard of me, so he thinks he's got it all figured out and that I know nothing.

He drops three more, bam, bam, bam. All three hit the back of the rim, slice through the net and come back to where he stands. The kid's got the touch—the ball comes back to him like a loyal pet. Takes arrogance to shoot that well, that pretty.

"Work left," I tell him.

Money drops two more. After the second, like the first, returns to him, he turns to me, ball cradled under his right elbow. "You been watching?" he says.

"I have."

"What are you seeing?"

"A big-league shot," I say and he smiles. "Going one way. You get half as good going left, you won't be here long."

"I won't be here long, coach. Only here to get the call."

"Then work left," I say. "And get someone to work with."

"I work alone," he says. "Not here to make friends."

"Did I say make friends?" The same stubbornness that makes him tough on the court makes him a pain in the ass to coach. "Never practice under conditions you don't see in a game. How many times a game are you wide open for a shot?"

"Never," he says and smiles. "If they've heard of me." He turns, takes one dribble, squares up and drops a twenty-five footer. An NBA three, plus a couple of feet. Hits the back rim and plunks down in the lane. The backspin carries it back to Money.

He shot it going right and I turn and walk away.

6

I MEET Terry at the Hob-Nob. Monday's his day off, he closes the Bunker, walks across the street and runs a tab outdoors.

"How's it going?" he says as I sit next to him.

There's a man singing at the street corner, his guitar case open, the acoustic strapped to his body by one of those leather weave belts that were popular in the 70's. Singing is the wrong word, really. The guy's lost most of his teeth and the words all come out sounding like a chainsaw played through a transistor radio. Bzzz, bzzz, bzzz. His playing is no better. The hand is an arthritically crippled claw and he doesn't play chords so much as he just slides his claw up and down the neck like a flesh capo. On the felt inside the open guitar case, it reads:

BILLY—LAST OF THE SIX-STRING OUTLAWS

I turn back to Terry, wonder why the six-string outlaw is here. Me and Terry are the only people at the bar—other than the waitress, who paints her nails and sneers whenever you ask her to get something— and it must be a hundred degrees.

"Been better," I say. I tell him about my trouble with Money. Tell him I think I could help the kid get to the pros, which is true, if he'd listen to me.

"Remember Dick Barnett?" I say.

"Any black man over 45 knows Skull Barnett," Terry says. "Played against him pre-season his last year with the Knicks. My first with the Stars. Salt Palace. He was an old man and he still torched me a couple times. Why?"

"Money shoots like him. Tucks his legs, looks like an upside-down question mark when he lets it go."

"Can he hit it like Barnett?"

I nod. "Better."

"And the rest of them?"

"Some listen, some don't. Hedda's got a great attitude, so far. Latimore's trying to stay straight."

"He's banned for one more year?"

I shake my head. "The ban's over. The NBA could have him if they wanted but no one'll touch him." I order a club soda and lime, wipe my sweat droplets off the bar with my arm. "No one thinks he'll stay clean."

Terry looks at me. "Will he?"

I take a drink. "Hope so."

"Know what you hope, Bomber. Do you think he will?"

He asks the question and I see Latimore ten years ago. We met at the Chicago pre-draft camps. A pro body at twenty, 6'10" 255 and quick as a guard. Best footwork I've ever scene on a big man, soft hands—hands that could cradle an egg dropped from the top of the Sears Tower. A first step that was an absolutely scary combination of power and finesse. A freight train that could pirouette. At that point, I'd been around the game for most of my twenty-three years, and I'd never seen a player like him. Still haven't. I was coming off my second major surgery and my second, and last, trip to the camps. I couldn't pay anyone for a tryout at that point.

Less than ten days after camp, I read that Darnell Latimore had tested positive for cocaine. His first, but not his last, slip. He would have been the first overall pick of the draft. I had science and hope holding together what was left of my knee and I hated Latimore.

I look straight ahead. "No," I say. "I doubt he'll make it."

"You know he won't," Terry says. He sips his ice coffee. "I played against Hedda's father, you know?"

"Really?"

"Charlie Davis. Strong forward. No Mel Daniels, but strong. You couldn't kick the ball out of his hands once he got a board."

"She's strong too," I say. "Plays bigger than she is."

The last of the six-string outlaws keeps singing. The words, the chords and notes, they have nothing to do with the original, but I think it's "You're Right, I'm Left, and She's Gone." I could be wrong, but I think that's the song I'm hearing behind his noise. Bzzz, twang, bzzz, twang.

"Shit," I say. "Doesn't that noise bother you?"

Terry nods, drinks his beer. "Every Monday it does, Bomber. You think I'm deaf?"

7

PUT YOURSELF in my shoes: Most of the years don't matter. Most of the days don't either. April first, 1980, you snap the anterior cruciate ligament of your right knee. Slice it badly enough that one side of your knee has nothing to do with the other side. April fools, but it's no joke. You feel it let go; the sound is a stick breaking. You think you've broken a bone—you haven't, it's much different than that and much worse. It's a ligament that you've never heard of and can't, for a while, pronounce correctly.

Most of the years don't matter. Most of the days don't either. April first, 1980, you snap the anterior cruciate ligament of your right knee. Slice it badly enough that one side of your knee has nothing to do with the other side. April fools, but it's no joke. You feel it let go; the sound is a stick breaking. You think you've broken a bone—you haven't, it's much different than that and much worse. It's a ligament that you've never heard of and can't, for a while, pronounce correctly.

The first surgery rebuilds the knee. Twelve months of rehab and your whole life is shaped by numbers. You do more work than you've ever done. Every day is the end of the world. Every day is exhaustion. It's all meaningless numbers for a year, every day. It starts with a wet towel—that's all you can lift—and you in a chair lifting your withered right leg. Two pounds. Five. Ten. Six months go by and you're up to eighty pounds, five hundred lifts a day.

This is not to make you better. It's to make you close—close, that's all you ask—to what you once were. And every day you wonder if it can work.

Another month and you're up to six hundred lifts. After a year, the knee still wobbles, doesn't support you laterally. A second surgery, cut deep and wide next to the other scars so that you now have five cuts to show off. Your doctor tells you your knee is as bad as Gus Johnson's, as bad as Mickey Mantle's. Could be as bad as Joe Namath's. He tells you this as if he's letting you into a special club, like it's good news.

Six more months go by. You support yourself by painting houses in the mornings. Afternoons, you go through more rehab—weights, runs and more leg lifts. Evenings, you shoot baskets and try to keep your touch. Your agent calls less often. The only time you see your name in the paper is past-tense—it's like you died. You'll make it back, you tell yourself. Nothing can stop you. You work the leg for six more months and it pops out at a summer league tryout for the Knicks.

Another year of rehab. No agent. You have to get your own try-outs.

Add the leg work to the rest of it that you've done every day all your life. Add it to three hundred sit-ups, fifty reps a pop, three hundred push-ups, fifty a pop, a hundred pull-ups. Three years with the leg. Before that ten years filled with bench presses, curls, flies, road work—thirty-five hundred days of work and sweat—all of it meaningless.

There are meaningful numbers that spin in your head and keep you awake.

A basketball court is 94 feet long and 50 feet wide and a fast player can run the length of it in 3.3 seconds. You did it in 3.1 three years and two surgeries ago. 94 feet in 3.1. A good day now, you're an arm hair under 4 flat. Three years ago you could take ten quarters off the top of the backboard—the top of the backboard is 13 feet even off the floor and it might as well be the Empire State Building now.

A forty-two inch vertical leap cut to twenty and no one needs to tell you the difference is more than twenty-two inches. The difference between 42" and 20" is the difference between the New York Knicks and painting houses with your brother-in-law for a living. It's planes instead of a Toyota Celica. It's two million a year or five hundred a week.

Numbers that add up. It's three years and two surgeries since you could trust your body. Trust your right knee. It's ninety-four feet that got longer and a backboard that got farther away and all the sit-ups and push-ups and rehab don't change that fact that what you were is not what you are. You're a thousand days older, half a second slower and twenty inches shorter.

You play for two days at the Chicago camps hoping to catch onto a European roster and no one will touch you. Every face at the camp looks at you with pity. You're one of those old men at the grocery store that pisses his pants in line. You're the reminder of what they might become with just one bad break. Eyes drop to the ground every time you look into them. Feet shuffle. Everyone has an excuse to not be around you. Three years, two knives, one ligament and you give up.

You paint houses, your wife finally leaves you and, for five years, you do little except drink and work. One day you quit drinking. You think it must've been some deep survival instinct, because it wasn't a choice. You didn't care. For seven years, you haven't cared about anything, and now you have a second chance and you care and you're scared.

You walked like a zombie through seven years of your life. The piece of you that cared was that truck tire you see on the side of the highway, blown off and dead.

You're in a hotel south of Sarasota bordered on three sides by chickenshit and the smell of burning manure and there is no way you'll sleep tonight. You'll stay up listening to Folsom Prison Blues and you'll hear the prisoners cheer every time Johnny Cash sings about shooting his woman down, sings about his Cocaine Blues, about shooting that man in Reno just to watch him die. The inmates, they'll cheer.

8

I GET to the gym early and walk around the court, dribbling every few feet, checking for dead spots. The bad news is that half of the court—the side away from the benches—is full of them, the wood puckered and bulged like blisters, which means Money will have to run off weak side screens for first half—strong side for the other. Put him on the bad side, it's like dribbling on the beach. The court's terrible. Welcome to the bush leagues.

For three quarters, neither team plays worth a shit and I'm embarrassed we've charged people money to see this. Latimore's rhythm looks off—he's thinking too much and it looks like he doesn't know what he wants to do or where he want to go. In basketball, there is no decision time; you do things. The defense reacts, you improvise. Latimore looks like he's taking dance lessons. He looks down a lot, stumbles, chases his brain all over the court. Mike Morris, our center, is a canned ham. Too slow to run, too small to play a power game. All night, he's slopped around like a dishrag by Tommy McClendon—a big kid from some junior college in Arkansas. After three, McClendon's got twenty points and eighteen boards. Five blocks. He's killing us. Two minutes into the fourth, Morris picks up his sixth foul and he's out of the game.

The only player I have doing anything is Money. He runs like a greyhound, comes off screens like Reggie Miller and he's been open all night. And open, he can't be stopped. Anything inside of twenty feet is a lay-up to Money. Seems like every play I call for him, he hits a shot. On offense, the kid makes me look like a genius. The down side is his man, a CBA re-tread named Teddy, or Terry—I forget which—Carlton, drives by him play after play, gets to the hole, and racks up fouls on my big men. With five minutes left, we're down three and I signal for a time-out.

"You're out," I say to Money when he starts to take a seat.

"What?"

"Get out of my huddle," I say. The other players stand around, looking back and forth, me to Money and back. I let him walk on me here, and the season's over. "Gates—play the two spot. Hedda, take the point."

"This is some fucking joke, right?" Money says.

"Darnell?" I say to Latimore. "How many fouls you have?"

Darnell holds up his hand, all fingers out.

"Five—and Morris is sitting next to me with six. I can't afford six on Latimore." Money is fuming—you can see that he'd like to kick my ass. "You're hurting the team."

"I got half the team's points," he says.

"And you gave that many back," I say. "Sit."

He turns and walks to the end of the bench, sits for a second, and stands. He kicks a water cooler, walks away from the bench and heads to the locker room.

Without Money, we fall behind by ten with a minute left. A total collapse. Hedda gets her pocket picked twice in a row. On the second, she hacks the guy that stripped her and they get a three-point play out of the deal. Three possessions in a row, we turn it over—three in a row, they score. Gates can't guard Carlton either, but at least he tries. With about thirty-five seconds left, Latimore fouls out on an over-the-back call. He comes toward the bench.

"Next time Darnell," I say.

"Right."

The game ticks away. Ten seconds. Five. We lose by sixteen.

Coach Ben Thompson. 0-1.

I sit. From behind the bench some fan is shouting at me. You suck, Thompson, he says. You're no coach. You're a drunken has-been. Without Money, you would have lost by fifty. I turn and look at the guy. Mid-thirties, about my age. Dressed nice enough. And I wonder: what did I do to deserve this? I must look like I'm going to say something, because Darnell grabs my arm and takes me away from the bench.

"Don't," he says. "It doesn't do any good."

I look at him. He's had ten years of these nuts yelling at him. Screaming at him like he'd killed people or something.

"I just wanted to know what possessed him to do that," I say as we leave the floor. "I'm not angry."

He walks by me, ducks at the door and heads into the locker room.

"You will be," he says.

Money's dressed and gone. I tell the team I'll talk with them to-morrow. No speeches tonight. When I announce that I'm not talking, Hedda gets up and heads to the women's locker room.

"Tomorrow," I say and walk out and head to the parking lot.

I get back to The Palms, and there's a note on my door. In a fin-ger-paint kind of smear, it reads:

Ben—Uncle Chicken wants to see you tomorrow. My sympathies— Bone.

9

"B EN THOMPSON, you look terrible," he says.

"Team looked worse," I say.

"You're too damn hard on yourself. Time to jell, son. That's what they need."

"We've only got twenty-seven more games," I say. "Sometimes, it takes longer than that."

"And, shit, boy—sometimes it takes shorter. You are the most nega-tive young man I have ever run across." He lights a cigar. "Look," he says. Parcell points to a large white cylinder on his desk—it's the color of an industrial toilet, the size of an import's hubcaps. He flicks a switch on its side and it starts to whirl like a small fan. Cigar smoke gets sucked down into the center. "New toy," he says. "Powerful. I lay this fucker down in Piccadilly Square and poof, London ain't foggy no more."

"Nice," I say.

"It's not nice," he says. "It's downright amazing, negative Ben Thompson. It's enough to sit in fucking awe at what human beings can achieve. An ashtray is one of the least important things on this planet, and look at that. The amount of thought and precision in a plastic piece of crap. Sit in awe, Ben Thompson. How in the hell did you ever become a great ballplayer?"

Ballplayer? The word throws me. No one says ballplayer—no one has for over twenty years. It hits me that Parcell might be older than I'd originally thought. "I wasn't always negative," I say. "I've grown into it."

"Well snap the fuck out of it. It's bad Karma for the team."

"Karma?" I say.

"What goes around comes around. Earthly balance and shit like that. Zen, son. I thought you did more than play ball in college. You haven't heard of it?"

"I have," I say. "I just wasn't aware that you were up on your Zen."

"I know very little Zen which, if I understand my Zen, means that I know a lot."

"I dated a Buddhist once," I say.

His intercom buzzes. Parcell's secretary announces that his cleaning service has arrived.

"Send her in," he says to the black box. He turns to me. "Don't make small talk with me, Ben Thompson. Tell me about my team."

"Your teams sucks," I say. "No center. No quality point guard. I've got Childs out of position at point—he's a two guard. Hedda's a power forward and I've got her backing up Childs. I've got a bunch of tweeners."

"Bunch of what?"

"Players with the body for one spot and the game for another. The pieces don't fit. Plus, there's no bench."

A young woman, maybe twenty-five, steps into the room with a milk-crate of cleaning supplies. She wears a white T-shirt with "Sarasota's Number One Cleaners" across the chest, white Nancy Sinatra hot pants with matching go-go boots and a pair of those yellow industrial gloves. The T-shirt, she takes off and, naked from the waist up, starts to clean the bar where Earl made the drinks the first day I came here.

"Hi, Mr. Parcell."

He nods. "Joanna."

I look at him.

"Topless cleaners. Sit in awe, Ben Thompson."

"You can get topless cleaners?" I say.

"You can get anything in this world," he says. "Sometimes you can't afford it, is all." He takes a drag of his cigar. "My team. Can you find me a center?"

I shake my head. "None to be had. The NBA doesn't have enough big talent to go around, then you've got the CBA and Europe ahead of us. Morris is a total zero, but he takes up space. I can use Latimore at center if I need to—he's got the size and he's quick. Could cause some match-up problems. A point, we might be able to find. Easier than a center. The bench is a bigger problem."

"Start the girl," he says and the cleaning woman turns around like she's listening.

"What does starting Hedda have to do with the bench?"

"It doesn't," he says. "But it puts fannies in the seats."

"So does winning," I say.

"And you can win with what you've got?"

Joanna moves over to the windows. She's beautiful and I feel sleazy for looking, but I don't stop. She stands up and gives me a look that says I-hope-you're-enjoying-yourself, you pathetic bastard.

"Can you win?" Parcell says.

I look back to him. "I think so."

"Better," he says. "Almost a positive attitude."

"If Money hasn't headed out of town by now."

"You haven't patched it up with him?"

"Not yet."

Joanna brushes behind Parcell and works on the big picture window. She reaches up, she's muscular and cut, her back shows no tan lines.

"Do it," he says.

I sit for a moment and try to think of what to say. Money may have taken off but, most likely, he's out at The Palms or on the court. This is his last chance and, like me or hate me, I hold his ticket up.

"Do it," Parcell says again. "Move. Good-bye. Go do your job, Ben Thompson."

I get up, head to the door. I turn and Parcell is showing off his new ashtray to the half-naked woman at his desk. He looks up, dismisses me with a wave of his hand.

"Make me proud," he says.

10

I GET BACK to The Palms and Bone has drained the pool. He's down at the bottom of the ten-foot end, and standing in ankle-deep water that looks like sewage. A siphon hose snakes around his feet and leads up under the diving board.

"Making paradise that much better," he says. "How'd it go with Uncle Chicken?"

"Did you know there were topless cleaners?" I say.

Bone looks up, shades his eyes. "I did."

"It was news to me," I say.

"A woman at school does it for extra cash."

"School?"

"Ringling School of art and design," he says.

"Ringling?" I say. "The circus."

"They're not affiliated," he says, sounding exasperated. "Mrs. Ringling was into art. Left a lot of money. Got nothing to do with the circus. It's an art school."

I nod, remembering the paint, the wall and the mess. "Right," I say. "You're a painter."

"Paint to relax," he says and shakes his head. "I'm primarily a sculptor. Found art. Check your garbage with me before you toss it. It'd be a favor."

I look down into the pool and take a seat on the diving board. Bone rolls out a white sealant on the bottom with an extender pole. Smells like Epoxy. "You need some help?"

"You're not allowed to help."

"Not allowed?"

"Uncle Chicken's orders. Through Earl. He thought you might want to paint, and he doesn't want you to."

Not allowed to paint. I'm not sure whether I should be mad at Parcell, or wonder where he's been all my life. Bone takes a couple steps back, the brown water holds his feet like mud. A suck and a release.

"Funky," I say.

He looks back up. "Would you believe shit was living in this?"

"Really?"

"Bugs, little things that look like frog babies. Prehistoric shit."

I get up, walk over toward the stairwell. "Guess something lives in everything," I say.

Bone stops rolling, looks up and smiles. "What the fuck does that mean?"

I stop. "Nothing. Gibberish. Have you seen Kenny Cash?"

"Which one's Kenny?"

"The mad one—last night at least."

"Haven't seen him."

I head up to my room and get my answer. On the bulletin board is a note: We need to talk. At The Bunker. It's signed with the dollar sign, $, underlined twice.

11

DOWN IN The Bunker, Money's shooting pool. It's dark and he wears sunglasses. If he sees me come in, he doesn't make a show of it.

"Your boy's pissed," Terry says as I get to the bar.

"Bad?"

"Bad enough. Thinks you're out to get him."

I take my club soda over to the pool table. Springsteen's "Open All Night" hums from the jukebox.

"We need to talk?" I say.

Money's playing nine-ball. He shoots, plants the seven and sets himself for the eight, and doesn't bother to look up. He shoots the eight, pulls back soft English and has the nine lined up.

"I'm here," I say.

He stands and looks at me. At least I think he's looking at me through the shades.

"I want to look at my EV's," he says.

I shake my head. "Why?"

"You're burying me," he says.

"I'm not."

"Let me see my EV's"

"EV's are for me and for scouts. You haven't even been scouted yet. Not here, anyway."

"And I won't get scouted if you give me a lousy evaluation no matter what numbers I put up." Money knocks the nine down and looks back up at me. "Let me see them."

"I won't, but I'll tell you what they say."

Money drops three quarters into the slots and the balls release and cascade down to my end of the table. I start to rack nine balls.

"So?" he says.

I look up at him, bent over from racking the balls. "They say everything I've said to you in practice. That you've got a killer shot—one of the best I've ever seen—going to your right. That you've got an explosive first step—going right. Good eyes—a good, but not great, passer. You're in great shape. Good rise, good stamina. That you've got the ability to be a decent pro defender, but you lack the wheels and desire to be a stopper."

"You know shit about my desire," he says.

"I'm basing it on what I've seen. Change my mind," I say. "We'd both be happy. You want me to finish?"

He sets the cue ball and stands there, not shooting. "Finish," he says.

"My analysis says that you're a one-armed player—one with game, but still a one-armed player—with an amazing spot-up J who happens to be a coach's nightmare."

"You put that in?"

"I haven't, but you're tempting me."

"But you haven't?"

"I haven't," I say. "But I will if you don't start listening to me."

Money gives me this I-don't-want-to-swallow-your-shit-but-I-will look. The kid hates authority. It got him into trouble in Italy; it's getting him into trouble here. But I can't blame him. Most coaches are no brighter or more informed than your average voter—it's best not to trust them or their opinions.

"Here's the deal," I say. "You start working your left and playing some defense and I guarantee you twenty to twenty-five shots a game.

Count eight or nine of those attempts as threes, and you should be at about thirty points a night." I can see he's listening, that I might have him hooked. "Thirty a night—in any league—talks a lot louder to scouts than my EV's."

"Twenty-five shots?" he says.

"Twenty to twenty-five. Don't get greedy."

Money looks calm; he's thinking it over. "Lenny Wilkens had no right," he says. "Couldn't stir a drink with his right hand, let alone dribble or shoot and he's in the Hall-Of-Fame."

"True. And Elgin Baylor couldn't punch out a baby with his left. That's them and this is you. That's the 60's and this is now. You want to get to someone's camp this fall? You want to get looked at?"

"You know it coach."

"Then do what I say. You'll put up numbers and the scouts will come. If they don't, me or Terry'll put in some calls."

"That old bartender?" Money says, pointing at Terry.

Terry doesn't seem to have heard. He's watching the silent TV over the bar. "Terry? How would you cover Money?"

Terry looks at the kid. "Force him left, sucker him into going right when I wanted. By half-time, he'd be asking me permission to shoot."

Money shakes his head like he's listening to two crazy people and walks past the bar toward the stairs.

"We got a deal?" I say as he heads up.

"Twenty-five shots a night, you bet your ass we got a deal." He's up the stairs and out. The light from the world outside comes into the stairwell and I see dust in the air. Then, it's dark again.

"You feel old talking like that?" Terry says.

"I do."

"Me too, Bomber."

12

OUTSIDE, the smell is incredible. The air reeks of shit and slaughter. On The Palm's side of the road are the two chicken farms that Parcell owns. Across the street is a small farm—

actually it's just a big yard with too many animals, which makes it something of a small farm—with a wooden hand-painted FRESH EGGS / MILK / FIREWOOD sign leaning up against the mailbox.

The chickens—the ones from the neighbor's farm, not Parcell's—run free over their lawn and I often find myself paralyzed waiting—literally—for chickens to cross the road.

The neighbor, who I've yet to meet, also has four or five cows. It's hard to tell how many for sure. I've seen four of them together and think there are five but—except for the blind one that bumps into our cars and the first floor apartments—they all look pretty much alike.

I walk the few blocks back from the Bunker. The smell, you don't get used to.

My car's dead. Nothing but a click when I turn the key. I've got two hours until practice and I'd rather not ride the team bus. It's best for the coach to stay away from the players when he can—living next to them challenges the balance too much as it is. You get too friendly, you lose authority. This is what I was told, what I was taught as a player, but I'm not sure I buy it a hundred percent.

Bone comes to the small parking lot. Hedda's with him.

"Problem?" Bone says.

I tell him. Turn the key a couple more times to prove my point. The second time, it doesn't even click.

"Where's your lug wrench?" Hedda says.

"Trunk maybe?" I say, not sure what a lug wrench is, but that's where all the tools are. I get out and walk to the trunk. The ground is spattered with chicken shit. Someone broke into my trunk a while back and the keyhole's gone. You can pop the latch with your finger.

She finds what she's looking for. "Get in," she says. "Turn it over when I say."

Hedda seems to know what she's doing so I get in. She gets under the hood and knocks the absolute shit out of something in the engine a couple of times.

Hit it? I'm thinking. Hell, I could've hit it.

"Give it a try," she says.

I turn the key, thinking this is stupid. That there's no way this could work. The car, it fires up and turns over.

Hedda comes to the driver-side window. "Your starter's going. Keep the wrench in the car. You'll need it to knock the starter until you get a new one."

I get out and she shows me where the starter is. "If it won't start, give it a couple of good whacks," she says.

"That'll work?" I say.

"For a while," she says. "Maybe six months, maybe six days. Eventually, you'll need a new one."

"We could go to Pick-a-Part," Bone says.

"No," I say. "I'll stick with it for a while." The tape deck only works if you stick a pack of matches in under the cassette. There are holes in both rear quarter panels. The windshield wipers cut out when it rains too hard. You hit a bump, the glovebox flops open. The muffler fell off when I banged it on some railroad tracks a couple of years back. It sounds like a big chainsaw. The muffler's in the trunk—I went back for it after it fell off.

The whole thing is a salute to entropy. This car's been with me a long time and I like its quirks. What's one more?

"Your call," Bone says.

"If it goes, Pick-a-Part will still be there," I say. I turn to Hedda and thank her. I get into the car.

"You going to practice?" she says.

I nod.

"Can I catch a ride? I wanted to talk with you," she says.

Hedda's wearing a pair of torn jeans and a T-shirt. Sandals. "I need to get going soon," I lie.

"Five minutes," she says. She starts toward the apartments. "I'll be right back."

I get out of the car again. The air-conditioning's been shot for years and it's torture unless you're in motion. I leave it running just in case the starter freezes up.

Bone watches Hedda climb the stairs and doesn't take his eyes off of her until she disappears into her room.

"Think I'm in love," he says. "Hedda's letting me do her tattoo."

"Really?" I say.

"Is that OK?" he says. "I mean, there's not a team rule about tattoos or anything?"

"I don't think I have any team rules," I say. Hedda comes out of her door. Bone watches her come down. "Tattooed Back-up Point Guard Descending a Staircase," I say.

"It'll be a beautiful piece of work," he says to me, like I have a lot invested in it.

Bone waves as we pull out of the lot, me checking the rear-view and Hedda turned around, both of us looking for chickens.

13

WE'RE HEADED NORTH up 441, the old Tamiami Trail—until the 70's the only road that connected Tampa to Miami. The Gulf's on the left of us, gleaming in the sun. A few jet-skis hop and fly on the water. Some old men fish off the pier. I wonder if they eat the fish—if they're safe or bloated with tumors like the ones you see on TV near the nuclear power plants.

"A tattoo?" I say.

"Don't worry," Hedda says. "After the season."

"I don't mind," I say. "Get it whenever you want."

"I'm thinking a big one. Some nice work. It'll take a while, and I'll have a lot of gauze. I'd look like Claude Rains."

"Gottcha," I say.

We practice at Sarasota High School. The games, we play on a worse court than the practice facility. School's out and Parcell got it somehow. I pull into the lot. A billboard—a big one, you can see it from 441 as you pull toward downtown—reads Sarasota Bengals-#1 in Florida. This is for the high school football team. It's a football state; they could give a rat's ass about basketball here.

Money's Kawasaki is already in the lot.

"You need to talk?" I say.

"Inside's cool," Hedda says as she gets out of the car.

"More private here," I say and point to Money's bike. There's a second helmet on it and I figure he brought someone. A good sign—maybe he's shooting over someone instead of working the empty gym.

Hedda grabs her bag from the backseat and shuts the door. She stands straight up.

"I want to play forward," she says.

"You're too small." She was a hell of a forward in college, but this is what I was worried about—she's used to being the star and if she plays here, it's got to be in a complementary role. I don't want to put her down, but I don't think she could handle playing the front court. "You don't have a forward's body."

"I'm 6'3"," she says.

"That doesn't prove me wrong," I say.

"Give me a shot."

"You're 6'3" and 185. You're a guard."

"I'm a forward," she says. "I'm getting killed in the back court."

Right now, I'd convert to any religion that could guarantee me happy players. I start to walk toward the gym.

"You're in a men's league," I say. "You knew it'd be tough."

"I thought I'd have a chance to fail at my own position," she says, following me. "Why did you draft me?"

"I didn't draft you, The Chicken Man did. You're here to sell tickets." When it comes out of my mouth, I regret it. Her face drops. She looks hurt, then angry. This is a truth she didn't need to know and it's my fault and it shouldn't have happened.

"Fuck you," she says and walks by me into the gym. She slams the door.

I look at my watch. Still an hour and a half before practice.

14

WHEN I GET out to the court, Money and Latimore are on one end going one-on-one. Hedda's running post-up drills, back to the basket moves. No noise, except gym sounds— grunts, the ping and mild echo of the ball bouncing off the floor and hitting the rim, the odd swish of the nets and the squeaks from the sneakers. I grab a ball from the rack and walk down toward Hedda.

"You should work against someone," I say.

"We're not talking," she says without stopping her drills. Drop-step up right, she grabs the ball, sets up on the other side of the paint, drop-step up left. She's sound fundamentally. Uses her body well, but it's hard to tell without someone on her.

"How'd you like to prove me wrong?" I say. I owe her this, but it can't hurt, either.

She stops and looks up. "I'd love to."

I blow the whistle and turn to Money and Latimore. I call them down to our end of the court. "Two-on-two," I say. "Darnell. Me and you against Money and Hedda."

"Me and a bunch of Pygmies," Darnell says. He rolls the ball he was using over to the sideline and looks at Hedda and Money. "Which of you dreamers is going to check me?"

"Hedda will," I say. "I'll take Money."

"I'll take Darnell," Money says.

"It wasn't a question," I say. "Me against you Money."

"You got to promise you don't bench me when I make you look silly," he says. He looks at Hedda. "Me and you against the old men."

"Looks that way," she says.

We shoot for outs. Money hits five straight and so do I. "We'll be here all day like this. What say the old men get it first?" I say. I'm thirty-four and I should be winding down a pro career. Darnell's twenty-eight and he should be starting in the all-star game. Next to these two, though, we're old.

"Whatever you say, coach," Money says. "You won't get it back."

He tosses me the ball and it hits me that this is my first pick-up game in nine years. I decide to play it safe and throw in to Darnell. He's on the right wing, about twenty feet from the hoop and I go to set a pick. He fakes right and Hedda stays with him. He comes back left, leads her into my pick. Money, like the lousy defensive player he is, doesn't tell her.

It doesn't matter. She makes contact with my chest and fights over the pick, staying with Darnell. Money switches, which he shouldn't have done, and I'm free. I roll to the hoop, call for the ball, and Darnell hits me in stride for a lay-up.

"One-zip, old men," I say.

I throw in to Darnell on the right side again. I make it look like the same play and come up to Hedda. Money calls the pick, but I don't set it. I hesitate for a moment and roll to the hoop. Hedda doesn't switch and Money recovers too late. I hit a reverse.

"Old men making you look silly," Darnell says.

"Wait till we get the ball," Money says.

"Not going to get it falling for sucker plays," Darnell says. He takes the ball in, tosses it to me on the left wing. Money's playing me straight-up, backed off a little and giving me the jumper. Darnell brings Hedda to the post, puts her on his back. I think she might front him, but she plays it right and the coach in me wants to give Darnell the ball and see how Hedda checks him. If she can play the post, this is a good test. The player in me wants to take Money to school. I'm a foot behind the three line and Money's begging me to take it—off me by four feet. I hit the J.

"Three zip," Darnell says, shaking his head.

"Shit, Money. Check him," Hedda says.

Darnell tosses in to me. I'm in the same spot and Money comes up tight. I give him a Chet Walker head-fake and he jumps out of the gym. I take a dribble into the lane, Hedda comes up on me and I give Darnell an alley-oop for a dunk.

"This is sad," Darnell says. He palms the ball in his right hand, and he puts his left up behind his ear. "You hear that, children? You hear the schoolbell ringing?"

"You haven't shown us shit, D," Money says.

I've got the ball at the top of the key.

"This is it, old man," Money says. "I gave you some nice memories, something for your scrapbook."

"You're going easy on me?" I say.

"Wrong tense, coach. I was going easy on you."

I fake a pass and take Money into the lane. He's still playing me straight-up. He should be playing me to go right. With my knee, I couldn't take Rose Kennedy into the paint going left and he should have spotted that by now. I'm worried that this kid might never catch on. I work him right and give him a little cross-over in the lane and take a ten foot fadeaway off my bad leg. The shot drops.

"That is one ugly fucking shot," Money says.

"Super John Williamson made a living with that shot," I say.

"Super who?"

"Great player. First guy I can remember who got kicked out of the league for getting fat. That up-the-ladder shot was his pet move."

He gives me the ball. "Ain't you the historian?" He gets in his defensive stance. "OK, Historian. You try your little Super Fat John Williams' move again."

I throw into Darnell and he toasts Hedda. Fakes her to the lane and blows by going right. He ends it with a reverse dunk.

He shakes his head again. "Coach, this is sad. Six-zip. Want to make seven a shutout?"

"Yes," Hedda says. "You score here, it's over." She looks at me and I can tell she's still pissed.

Darnell throws to me. I fake right and spin back left. But I'm slower, much slower, than I thought and Money's waiting for me. He strips me, takes a dribble in the lane and throws it down.

"This shit is over," he says. "OVER." He's at the top of the key. I get down, knowing he wants the jumper going right. But I overcompensate, and he's by me left. Darnell switches. Money feeds Hedda for a ten-footer and she hits it off glass.

Money struts back to the top of the key.

"Stop the presses," Darnell says, laughing. "You scored."

"One of many to come, D. You ready old man?" he says to me. I nod, play him a shade over to the left. He hits a three with my hand in his face. The kid has a gorgeous shot. The upper body's straight as a board, the legs go into that weird Barnett tuck. Perfect balance, perfect rotation. I'm tired and winded. The muscles around my bad knee quiver.

Money drains two more jumpers, both squared-up, both with a hand in his face. Hedda takes Darnell off the dribble. She can create her own shot, which is a good sign.

"Six-all, chumps," Money says. "Do you feel it, coach? Do you feel the momentum changing?" He tosses in to Hedda. I try to check Money, but I want to see what Hedda does with a big man on her. She works Darnell to the post, backs him in and gives him a pretty up-and-under move and hit it off glass. Money worked inside of me—if there was a rebound, it would have been his. He takes the ball as it comes through the net.

"Seven," Money says. "And counting."

My leg gets more wobbly and my wind gets shorter. I feel old and stupid. Money plays with me like a playground chump. It's getting near practice and the rest of the team starts to trickle in. Hedda and Money are up 15-6 and it gets uglier with each possession. Hedda's holding her own with Darnell and, while I'm impressed with her, I wonder what's wrong with him. All the tools are still there, but he's a beat slow, just like in the game the other night. But it's me, and not Darnell, that got us in this hole.

Money's out on the wing. He jab-steps me and I can see he wants to go right. The last few, he's taken me left and he thinks he's got me set-up. But I try to make him go left. Another jab-step.

"You watching, Coach? This is gonna be pretty." He gives me an up-fake and I bite. He's gone before I reach the ground.

We get it back and Darnell hits a few. It's time for practice and we're down 20-9. Money has the ball at the top of the key.

"I'm going right," he says. "I'm telling you to make it fair. I won't even fake you, Coach. I'm going right, you ready?"

I nod and get down in my stance.

"You hear me?" Money says. "Going right. Right by the coach, and right over you, D." He's dribbling at the top of the key and he smiles and turns to the team gathered at the side of the court. "Around him," he says and points at me with his free hand. "And over him." He points at Darnell. "Everybody with me?"

"So let's see it," Morris says from the side.

They may see it all of it, but I don't. Money's by me like a blur. By the time I turn, he's dunking over Darnell. Grace and power—a beautiful move.

Money hangs on the rim and does a chin-up. He comes down, and shakes hands with Hedda. He walks toward the locker room.

"I'm so good, even I can't stop me," he shouts.

"Five minutes," I say. "Back on the court in five, Money."

He nods, gives me a wave without turning around, and heads inside.

Hedda comes over to me. "Well?"

"You looked good." She gives me an arrogant smile and walks away. "I'm sorry," I say as she turns into the women's locker room.

"You, too," I say. "Five minutes."

15

BY THE TIME I get back home, my entire body aches. What I'd like is a twelve-pack and a Percodan, but I settle for a hot bath. I'm getting adjusted to the water and the phone rings. I decide to let it go. After the third tone, an answering machine—which I don't have—kicks in, and Rube Parcell's voice answers my phone.

"Ben Thompson is not in at the moment. Please state your business, time of call and phone number, and he'll get back to you as soon as he can. If you're calling about Sarasota Sun tickets, dial 1-800-SARASUN for the most exciting action on the coast."

I'm still in the tub when Parcell's voice comes back on the machine.

"Ben Thompson? I didn't put this in so you could screen me out. Pick up the god damn phone." He waits a couple of seconds. I can hear the whirl of his new ashtray in the background. "Hell," Parcell says. "Call me as soon as you get in."

I get out of the tub and throw some shorts on. Bone's down by the pool. He's got some tarp spread—it looks like a flattened out circus tent—and he's spray painting the body of an old lawnmower. I call his name a couple of times, but he doesn't respond. I walk down to him.

"Bone," I say when I get next to him. He's down in a catcher's stance. He looks up and turns, forgetting to shut off the nozzle. My leg gets a fine mist of Forest Green.

"Fuck," I say, moving away from him and shaking my leg like a cat that stepped in water.

He shuts off the gun and stands. "Sorry. I get kind of lost when I'm working."

I start to wipe the paint off, but all it does is smear it around. I shake my head. "I'll live," I say. "I've had a lot of paint on me over the years."

"That's right," he says. "I forgot."

"Was Parcell around here today?"

He nods. "Wanted me to put an answering machine in your room."

"So you knew about it?"

"Once he got here, I did." Bone bends down and puts the spray gun in a bucket of water. He turns it upside-down and clears the nozzle.

"And you did it?" I say. "That's my room."

"Case you haven't noticed, I live here for free and I don't do a hell of a lot. It's a good deal. Uncle Chicken calls, I got to answer." He shrugs.

I'm angry enough to hit something, but I realize it's not Bone's fault. "OK. Just let me know if you need to get in my room?"

"I would've," he says. "It wasn't my decision."

I nod and head upstairs, hoping to catch Parcell before he leaves the office. On the machine are three more calls, all from The Chicken Man.

16

PARCELL WANTS a meeting with me—won't talk about it on the phone—so I drive north to Tampa. "You're calling me?" I say.

"I wanted to talk about my team," he says with a big grin. "Where the hell have you been?"

"Working. With your team." I take a seat and wince. My knee is stiff and I don't have any power in it. I want to bend it, I've got to grab the ankle and maneuver it into position. It cracks and pops like walnuts in a vise grip.

"Jesus Christ. Did that noise come out of you, Ben Thompson?"

"Played a little pick-up with Hedda, Money and Darnell. Think I put some fluid on it."

"Get that taken care of," Parcell says.

"It has been," I say. "A few surgeries ago." What it needs now is to be drained. Parcell unwraps a cigar and looks at it. I'm thinking about the needle, four inches long, they stick under the kneecap. They hit the pocket, and suck out this pink mix of blood and pus. It shoots and swirls into the hypo and just thinking about it, I get queasy. I decide to rest it. I shake my head. "I'm out of shape. It shouldn't hurt like this."

"Go to one of my gyms," he says. "I'll comp it. Anything for my coach."

"I might," I say. "Right now, it needs rest."

Parcell lights his cigar. "What do you know about Lewie Keller?"

"Nothing. Who is he?"

"A ballplayer. Point guard. Do you want him?"

"How the hell should I know?"

"You need a point guard. You said so yourself. Now, who are you willing to give up?"

"Slow down," I say. "This isn't mail-order. These are players. One, they're not interchangeable. I don't need just any point, I need the right one. Two, you don't trade blind. I'd like to see the kid."

"Fine. I'll put you on the plane. Just say when," Parcell says. Behind him, I can see it's raining, which it does every day at four o'clock. You could set a watch by it. August. Florida. Rain. Four in the afternoon. It's always done in less than ten minutes.

I shake my head. "I don't have a free day. We're up in Baton Rouge tomorrow night."

"The Swamp Devils?" Parcell says.

"Dragons, I think." I shrug. "Could be Devils. We've got them in a home and home. Up there tomorrow, back here in three days. I can't look at the kid. What do you know about him?"

"His agent called me. Said Keller's quick and a good defender, but he's stuck behind some other point in Mobile."

"His agent called? He might not even be available. Have you talked to the team?"

"All taken care of. I almost traded for him this afternoon. But they wanted Grant and Latimore. I thought I should talk to you about it."

I shake my head and look past Parcell and out the window.

"What's the matter?" he says.

"I can't work like this. You put machines in my house, you tell me how to run the team."

"Machines? Hell, boy, it's an answering machine. You make it sound evil. What the fuck are you? Amish or something? And you're god damn right I tell you how to run my team."

I run my hand over the knee. I can feel the swelling, the years of abuse. It's like I'm feeling every weight, every mile all at one moment. And I thought I wanted more of this game. "I quit."

"You're under contract," Parcell says calmly.

"Sue me. You'll get a Toyota. I don't need this shit. Taking basketball advice from Colonel Sanders."

Parcell looks at me and puffs of his cigar. He's mad, but he's holding back. "I'll forgive that, Ben Thompson, because it's the first fight I've seen in you. You rent that spine, or is it here to stay?"

"I'm done," I say.

"The hell you are. Here's the deal. You call the shots on the floor. You let me know what players you need and I'll get them and then stay out of it."

"Too easy," I say. "What do you get out of this?"

Parcell laughs. "Ben Thompson, I already got it. You fought back. I pushed and you pushed back. That's all I wanted. For you to stand up and act like a man."

A quick hustle. And I feel like an idiot. I could still quit, but I got what I wanted. Even if he played me, I got it. I'm thinking of the few times on the court when I knew I was outclassed. The easy route is to walk—the hard one is to stick around and learn something. "Deal," I say. "But only if you stick to your end."

"Of course." Parcell walks over to the bar. "You still need a point guard, and I know of one available. Assuming it's all right to suggest one to you. How will we get a look at Keller?"

"Terry Willis," I say. "If the money's right, I could ask Terry to take a look."

"The money's right, Ben Thompson. I'll pay Willis more to look at him than I pay you to coach, if that's what it takes."

I look up at him. "Really?"

"I get what I want," he says. "You trust Willis' opinion?"

"He scouted me out of high school. Played pro. He knows the game."

"Done," Parcell says. "We'll get him some tickets." He pours himself a drink. "Go home, Ben. You look tired as hell."

I work my way out of the chair and limp toward the door. The knee makes a squishy noise from the inside with every bend.

"Ben Thompson," Parcell says. I turn around as I reach the door. "I'm proud of you." He smiles and, like a stupid kid, I smile back. "But I was serious about ripping your trachea out. You fuck with me or push the chicken jokes too far and you'll leave this town on a stretcher." He gives me a toast with his glass. "But, hell, you're close to a stretcher on your own. Don't need my help, do you?" He gives me that wave of his and I leave.

17

IT'S TOO HOT to touch my steering wheel when I get down to my car. The rain here, it does no good. It swoops in, makes the world wet for ten minutes, and leaves everything as it was. A tape—Jonathan Richman and the Modern Lovers Rockin' and Romance—has melted on the dash. I look back up the mirrored glass skyscraper and try to place Parcell's office. He's hovering up there on the thirty-third floor, running a good chunk of Florida, and my life. I lose count starting from the bottom three times. The heat makes me dizzy and the sun's glare off the mirrored glass hurts my eyes. I get in my car and use a T-shirt from the back seat on the wheel. My parking gets validated and I make some turns out of Tampa until I'm on I-75 and headed south to The Palms.

The drive takes about an hour and I spend it thinking about whether or not I should have quit. Parcell scares the hell out of me. The recurring trachea theme is disturbing—he's old enough to have served in Korea—and it's possible that his toughness isn't all talk. I decide to try and stay on his good side. I'm still not sure how I got there, but it seems I'm there.

A little after six, I turn off 41 and head home. At the corner where The Bunker sits is the guy I saw playing guitar and singing at the Hob Nob. It's Billy, The Last of the Six-String Outlaws holding a sign and marching back and forth in front of Terry's bar. I slow the car down to read it. As the car comes to a stop, he looks right at me, walks toward the car and thrusts the sign forward. I figure it's one of those "Will Work For Food" signs you see that always leave you flat and helpless and sad.

Safer a Picnic in Zagreb than Urological Surgery at Sister's Hospital

Billy holds it closer to my car like he wants some kind of response. There's not a hospital for miles, and I wonder why he chose Terry's bar for his soapbox. I hit the gas and pull away.

It takes me about five times longer than normal to get out of my car. This is how you'll feel every day in ten years—twenty if you're lucky—I tell myself as I climb up the stairs to go to bed. I drag the leg out to the side because it won't bend enough to take the steps straight on. Every day, you'll feel like this.

18

I CAN'T SLEEP most of the night with my leg throbbing. I stay up, thinking about all the nights this knee has cost me. After the first surgery, they stitched it up wrong, or put the plaster on too tight—they were never sure which it was—and I rolled over in my sleep in the hip to ankle cast. It popped some of the stitches and the knee hemorrhaged. Spread a pool of dark blood through the cast. We popped a couple more bending and twisting me into the car and the cast was a deep purple by the time Linda got me to the hospital. Blood from the inside is a different color than a simple cut—it oozes thick and oily in a blackish-purple. Once, when I still drank, I threw up the same color into a toilet in some Montreal bar.

The sun comes up and I sit out on the porch with some coffee and watch it. At seven, I go down to Bone's chair by the still-empty pool and start my EV's. They're these sheets that chart the strengths and weakness of a player. You rate them on a one to ten scale—ten being the top. I look down at Money's. You've got to fill in the blanks relating to the player's physique, speed, jumping ability, quickness of hands, stamina, shot and intangibles and so on. Then, you answer LIKE WHO? Describing them isn't what the scouts and the teams want—they want a shorthand note of who the kid's like. I still have some of my old EV's—I got them from my last agent before he let me go. A scout once said Walt Frazier in my Like Who column for defense. Me and Walt Frazier in the same sentence.

I tap my pencil on the clipboard; too tired to fill in the pages. My head is full of sand, so I sit and feel the sun heat me up for a while.

At eight, I head to The Bunker. Terry opens early, but there are rarely customers before the noon crowd. He spends most of his mornings reading papers. Terry's a news junkie—we'd go on road trips when I was at Miami, and he'd buy up all the newspapers he could find and read them all standing up. The guy never sat—he'd even eat room service standing up, reading the whole time.

I work my way down the stairs. The knee won't bend, so I drop the right leg on a stair, support myself with my hand on the railing, and release the rest of me down after the bad leg. I put pressure on the right leg, and it's like there's crushed glass tumbling in there. Any motion or weight, and I wince. I'm about half way down and Terry comes to the bottom of the stairs.

"Didn't I used to be older than you?" He climbs up and helps me down. We reach the floor and I pat him on the back and hug him up by the neck.

"Once upon a time," I say. "It's not as bad as it looks. Just some fluid."

"You're sure? Nothing popped?"

"If it did, I didn't hear it," I say. "Always have before."

He helps me to a stool and gets me some coffee.

"Your boss called me," he says.

I nod. "Can you do it?"

"I'm no one's charity case, Bomber." He takes a drink and stares at me over his mug.

"I don't follow you."

"I'm doing fine here—don't need no help."

"You got it backwards," I say. "I need your help. I'm trying to make a go of this, and I need a point."

He shakes his head. "I don't buy it. Great white father offers me a ton of money to look, just look, at some kid in Mobile? Scouting trip ain't worth more than a couple hundred—it's a one day gig—and this man calls me this morning and says your chicken king is going to drop two grand on the deal. Shit ain't right."

"Two grand?" I say.

The bar is quiet except for our breathing and the pops and gurgles of the coffee maker. "Don't tell me you didn't know."

I shake my head.

"Bullshit," Terry says.

I do my best to fill him in on how little I know. It takes a couple minutes for me to prove how inept and powerless I am.

"Sorry," he says. "Thought I was getting a pity fuck."

"Better than none at all," I say.

"I would've taken the job." He smiles. "But I had to let you know I was hurt."

"So you'll look at Keller?"

"I'll look," he says. "But what kind of strings are there? What if the kid's a zero?"

I shrug. "We don't make the trade."

"So he's serious? Two grand to scout the kid?"

"If that's what he said," I say.

"Parcell for real?" Terry says.

"In his own way, he is. Like I said, I don't know a whole lot more about Parcell than you. He knows a little about the game, but not much. He's got to be losing a ton of money on it. It seems like a game to him."

"It is a game," Terry says.

"A different game, if you know what I mean. I'm like a pet—the team's a toy to play with."

"He's an owner," Terry says. "That's the way they are."

I nod and feel a little stupid for agreeing. Parcell is my first owner. Terry dealt with a few, but I had no idea what to expect and I'm still off-guard at every turn. "You got a satellite dish, right?"

"Got one. Don't know shit about using it, but I got one."

"We're on some shitty little sports network tonight. Can you tape it?"

Terry agrees and I drag my body to the airport. Parcell may be nuts and hard to deal with, but we go—on this trip at least—in style. The Sarasota Sun—the only Gulf Coast League team that flies—meets me at the airport.

19

COACH BEN THOMPSON went 0-2 in Baton Rogue. This time, there's no one to blame but me. Latimore finally looked the player he used to be—26 points 16 boards and a bunch of blocks. Ran the floor pretty well until he gassed out in the fourth. Money hit for thirty. But I fucked up. Before the game, I run into Chucky "Hoops" Chandler—a CBA and freelance NBA scout. If Chucky's here, he's not alone. Scouts are like cockroaches—you see one, you've got a nest. He's slime, but his word carries weight. Chucky Hoops is looking for players so I go to Clem Garret, coach of the Swamp Dragons while the players are running warm-ups.

"Listen," I say to Garret. "We've got some eyes on the guys tonight."

We're by the scorer's table, our teams run lay-up drills, except for Latimore and Anthony Walker—another re-hab case that should be in the bigs—who talk at center court in the jump circle. "I know," Garret says. "What do you want?"

"No zones. Straight man. We throw zones at each other, and there's no way Chucky or anyone else has an accurate report. What do you say?"

"I hate zones," Garret says and gives me a just-sucked-lemons face. His dentures don't fit right—they're too big and kind of flappy—

and his mouth looks mildly tortured. Lon Chaney talking hoops. "Rat-ass league shouldn't allow it. Fine with me."

The game's tight all the way. Money and Darnell play well enough for it to matter. We're in a position to win and my two best players look solid in front of the scouts. Everything's about as good as I could have hoped. We're down one with fifteen seconds left and I burn my last time-out to set up a play.

I set a two-man screen and roll with Money and Latimore and I never saw it coming. Out of the time-out, Garret throws a box-in-one zone on us. They face-guard Money and Gates can't get the ball in. We turn it over, they hit a shot, and we lose.

"What the fuck was that all about?" I say to Garret as he heads to his lockers. "We had a deal."

"And I kept it. You wanted your guys to look good and they did. You got your deal," he says. "Your players looked fine. Only their coach looked bad."

I grab his jacket and swing him in front of me. I could hit him; head-butt him. I can see his forehead splitting open, feel his blood on my face. Darnell comes up behind me, and starts to pull me away.

"Fuck you, Thompson," Garret says and swings free of my grasp.

"Calm down, coach," Latimore says and takes me off the court.

On the plane home, I stand up in the center aisle like I'm about to show them how to breathe into those masks. "My fault," I say. "I owe you one." The borderline players, they don't seem to care much—this is their last stop and they're inching closer to selling insurance or aluminum siding or painting or tending bar. The players who've been somewhere, though, Gates, Darnell, Money and Hedda, I'm losing them.

Ben Thompson, loser, sucker, 0-2 chump, sat down, his leg straight and obtrusive in the aisle.

20

TERRY MEETS ME, to my surprise, at the airport.

"The kid's a keeper," he says.

"You've seen him?"

He nods as he steers. "Fast and quick. Good court sense. No shot." We get to the ticket booth. "On me," he says. "And dinner if you want it."

"You tape the game?"

"I set it to. Had to fly out to Mobile."

We grab some take-out Chinese and go to The Bunker to watch the game. From what Terry says, Keller's good enough to trade for. I want Terry to see the team and get his ideas on who we can let go of. We're into the second quarter; Terry stands behind the bar and I'm on a stool.

"Cash went left," he says as Money cuts around a screen up on the TV.

"Not well," I say. "But he's mixing it up a little."

Terry watches the TV, and doesn't look at me when he talks. "A good point'll help him. He's working too hard. Ball's in his hands too much."

"I'm doing what I can," I say.

"No offense, Bomber. They look pretty good—it wasn't a criticism. You seem to have a fix on it."

At half-time, Terry fast forwards the tape with the remote in his right hand while eating with his left. Half-time zips by with some three-point shot contest and bunch of dancing cheerleaders in spandex tights. They move, all jerky and funny, synchronized in spastic movement.

"What's the deal with the six-string outlaw?" I say.

"Safer a picnic in Zagreb?" Terry says. "Got me. Sisters Mercy is downtown."

"Why's he outside The Bunker?"

"He's got to be somewhere," Terry says. "Odd sign though." He stops the tape, and cues it up for the third quarter. "Demands an awful lot from its audience. Got to know a little about sentence construction and world events."

"He's asking too much," I say.

"Around here, he is. Sound like he's got a story to tell. Man walks around with a sign like that, he's begging you to ask what's up."

"Did you?" I say.

He shakes his head. "Just cause he's begging don't mean I got to ask. Listening to people's trouble's like feeding stray dogs, Bomber."

The game is on again. Latimore has a beautiful third—he's all over the court on defense, rotates well and runs in transition. He's out on the right wing—his strong side. If Latimore goes right, he's going all the way to the hoop. If he goes left, he takes a ten foot jumper.

That's his only bad tendency—it's too predictable. But Tony Capel, the guy who's guarding him, can't stop him either way.

On the tape, Latimore throws a ball fake with one hand. He palms the ball like it's a grapefruit and makes like he's hitting a cutter in the lane. Capel bites the fake, Darnell blows by him right and dunks.

"Pretty," Terry says. "Connie Hawkins."

I nod. "Kids today think Jordan invented that."

"Kids today think a lot of shit," he says.

Latimore makes a steal and flies down the left wing. He's got a chance for the lane, but he makes the right pass and hits Money spotting up for a three.

Terry whistles. "Boy can shoot." He rewinds the play back to Latimore's steal and watches it again. "Latimore doesn't play like he's selfish."

"He's not," I say. "Team player. Good kid."

"He's not selfish," Terry says and laughs. "He's a fuck-up. You dangle ten million in his face—which is fuck you money, be somebody money—and what does he do? Runs to a dealer and puts it up his nose, in his veins, or however the fuck he did it." Terry pauses the tape and looks at me.

"He's clean," I say. "He's hanging in."

"Clean, shit," he says. "Don't do it. Don't count on this kid. Don't trust him and don't care about him."

"You don't know him," I say.

Terry goes back to his food. He eats out of the little box they give you. They've changed them, those boxes. No more metal handles so now you can toss them in a microwave. Terry points at me with his chopsticks. "Spencer Haywood. Michael Ray Richardson. Terry Furlow. Roy Tarpley," he says. "Learn from history."

The list is a who's-who of ruined careers. Furlow, they found OD'd on heroin in a car accident after his fourth year. I add to the list in my head. Bubble Hawkins, a sweet lefty shooting guard that got a shot with the Nets in '77 when Tiny Archibald popped his Achilles, dead in a crack house in Detroit last winter. Marvin "Bad News" Barnes, flushed out of the league in four years with Hall of Fame talent.

"Haywood cleaned up," I say. "So did Barnes. Richardson—he's still playing in Europe. Bernard King."

"King was alcohol," Terry says. "So were you, Bomber. That's different."

"Don't go there," I say. My body squeezes itself up cold and tight. "You don't know Latimore, and you don't know addiction. Staying straight is harder than coming off an injury. It's worse than divorce. It's with you every day, sometimes down to the minute. You've got no right to talk about it."

Terry shakes his head and puts his food on the counter. "I don't want to fight you. And if I crossed a line, I'm sorry. But I know I'm right. He's dead weight. Cut him loose. Trade him for Keller."

"He's worth three Kellers," I say.

"Ten years and a million miles ago, he was. Trade him," Terry says. "You know you should."

I shake my head.

"What do you owe him?" Terry says.

"Maybe nothing," I say.

"Don't give me that brotherhood of fuck-ups garbage," he says.

"I owe him a chance. I owe myself a chance to help him."

Terry dumps an empty box of food into the trash. He comes from behind the bar and goes toward the men's room. He stops by the pool table. "You won't trade him?"

I shake my head. "I'm thinking Morris and Gates."

Terry tosses the cue ball from one hand to the other. He nods. "That's the second best deal you could make. The kid's got game, but they'll take Morris and Gates." He drops the ball in a pocket. "We OK, Bomber?"

"Just a difference of opinion."

He opens the door to the men's room. "I'll be right out. Keep the tape paused."

I look up at the tape, stopped after Darnell's steal and Money's three-pointer. They're together, high-fiving at midcourt. I watch them, frozen in their minor celebration, until Terry comes back.

Early in the fourth quarter, we're up six. Things are clicking and the momentum's with us.

"Thought you lost this game," Terry says.

"We did. Darnell gets tired, and our spacing goes downhill. Bad execution." As if on cue, Darnell floats a lazy pass out of a double team and they get two in transition.

The last play happens—they score after our turnover—and the little me on screen goes nuts. What seemed like legitimate anger to me when it happened looks like a crazy person on the TV. I jump up and down, stomp my foot like a spoiled kid. My face is red and I'm screaming at Garret.

"What the hell happened to you?" Terry says.

I hold up my hand to shush him. You can hear my voice, booming and distant at the same time, from the courtside mikes.

"Totally unprofessional behavior," the play-by-play guy says. "Thompson ought to be ashamed of himself. It's sad that a great game has to end this ugly."

Terry pauses the tape with me screaming at Garret and Darnell just about to take me away. I shrug. "He said he wouldn't throw a zone at us. I lost my cool."

"That you did," Terry says. "You got to learn to take these things less personal."

I look back up at crazy me fixed on the screen. I smile, embarrassed. Terry hits play and the announcer comes back on.

"Ben Thompson was a fine player," he says. "But he has an awful lot to learn about coaching."

"Chump probably never picked up a ball," Terry says. He's trying to be nice, but the guy's right.

"Didn't need to," I say.

21

I CALL Parcell in the morning and it's a done deal. We get Keller and they get Gates, who's seen his best days, and Morris, who can't play. A steal. The kid's on a plane and we should get him for the afternoon practice. He'll start tomorrow night.

"Went easy?" I ask Parcell.

"Easy enough," he says. "Nothing for you to worry about, Ben Thompson. We had to throw in a meat freezer."

"What?"

"Keller's got three kids. His wife wanted a new meat freezer. I threw in an old one from one of the chicken houses. Everybody's happy, Ben Thompson. Gates and Morris can pick up their tickets at the airport after you let them know." He hangs up.

I was feeling great—sun on your face, rings tapping on the steering wheel great—until Parcell reminded me about Gates and Morris.

All the time we talked about the deal, it didn't hit me until now that it's my job, my responsibility, to tell them. I pace for a while. I clean my room. When I'm done, I look around to see if there's anything else I can do to put it off. Finally, I walk to Gates' room.

"Steve," I say after I close the door behind me. "This is the hardest thing a coach has to do." Sentence after sentence trips, club-footed, out of my mouth and it hits me that these aren't my words. It's a script—what my USBL coach said to me the last time I was cut. Gates interrupts me.

"What was the deal?"

I tell him.

Gates shakes his head and looks down at the floor. He wipes his face and it seems like he's about to cry. And I can't blame him. He's been around and he knows what this means.

"The short end of a two-for-one," he says. "In the Gulf Coast League." He takes a deep breath and nods. "Mobile got a shooting guard?"

"Cornell Maclain," I say. "I wish they didn't, but they do." I look down at the floor. There are coffee stains on the rug. Gates was a hell of a two-guard before he lost the knee. "Steve. I know where you are." I point at my leg.

He puts up his hand. "Don't," he says. "I know you're trying." He takes another deep breath and starts to shake a little. "Just get the fuck out." He speaks slowly and deliberately. He looks up at me. "Get out."

I shake my head and head out the door. I close it and take a few steps towards Morris' room and I hear something smash against a wall.

"Fuck," he screams. Another smash. And then it's quiet.

22

MORRIS GOES easier. He's a lummox, happy to have a job. Still, I feel awful. I've told two people they have no future in twenty minutes. I need to pass on some good news and I knock on Hedda's door.

"We made a deal," I tell her. "You're starting at small forward tomorrow night."

She laces her sneakers—she's started dressing in her room, instead of at the gym. She looks up at me.

"Who's gone?"

"Morris and Gates for a point. You're at small, I'm moving Grant to power and Darnell to the middle."

"I can play in this league," she says.

"I hope so. You've got your chance."

She stands. "This isn't because you owe me?"

"Does it matter?" I say

"No."

"I'll see you at practice," I say and go down to my car feeling heavy and slow. I look back up at the second floor and Gates is out of his room with two packed bags. I get in the car and turn the key. It's dead. I pop the hood, knock the starter a couple of times and try it again. I look up and Gates is gone—either back in his room or down the stairs.

23

I DECIDE TO take Parcell up on his offer to work out in one of his gyms. My leg is shot for a while—I can't run, so I might as well work the upper body. I wait at the counter behind some guy in a business suit. He moves on and I limp up to the desk.

"I don't have a membership," I say. "But Rube Parcell said I could work out here."

As soon as I say Parcell's name, there's paperwork in front of me. "You're his basketball coach?" the clerk says. She says it like you're his suitcase.

"Yes," I say. I end up with two months free with full privileges.

"Let us know if there's anything we can do for you, Mr. Thompson," she says. I thank her and walk to the locker room, thinking things could be worse—I could be someone else's suitcase.

I go through the motions on the weight machines. Staying healthy never made a whole lot of sense to me after all the rehab. I worked so many machines in my life with one goal in mind—to get the leg back—that they seem pointless to me. Even now, though, running straight for the sauna makes me feel like I'm cheating somehow. I finish some curls and move over to the bench press.

On the machine is Parcell's topless cleaner. "Hi," I say.

She doesn't break her rhythm and pumps out twelve more as I watch. She's cut and defined and sweaty. She gets to a sitting position.

"All yours," she says and gets up.

"We met at Rube Parcell's office, didn't we?" I say. She turns and looks at me. "Joanna? You were cleaning."

"Right and wrong," she says. "Look, I come here to be alone and I'm in the middle of something, OK?"

"Sorry," I say and she walks over the rowing machine. I stare at her ass and legs as she walks away. She stops and turns around.

"Getting a good look?"

I look down and get to work on the bench press.

24

LEWIE KELLER is as quick as a waterbug. He's going two-on-two—teamed with Hedda against Darnell and Money—and he's blowing by Money every time. Nice crossover, great spring. I watch him hit Hedda—he leads her beautifully on a switch and she powers in for a lay-up. Terry's right, the kid's a player.

Money gives Keller space and he dribbles out high. He jab-steps twice to the left and Money doesn't bite. Hedda calls for the ball on the post, but Darnell's behind her and Money's shaded over. Keller should take the jumper, but he dribbles out on the post and looks to the lane. Money stays back with Hedda, daring him to take the shot.

Keller, reluctantly, takes the J and I see why we got him so cheaply. Terry said his jumper was weak, but it's the most pathetic excuse for a shot I've seen in years. Comes out of his hands like a line-drive knuckleball. It pounces off the back of the rim like it was shot out of a cannon and comes back to Keller twenty feet out. Money chased the ball off the boards and that's all the daylight Keller needed. He cuts down the lane and dunks with one hand before Darnell can make the switch.

Darnell's got a sore Achilles and I wonder if he's pushing too hard. I blow the whistle and walk over to Keller.

"Take five," I say and shake Keller's hand and introduce myself.

"Do we really fly to away games?" Keller says.

"Sometimes we do," I say and he looks impressed. He should be—it's unheard of for the bush leagues to fly and Parcell drops money left and right for a team that's yet to win a game. I wonder when local legend Ben Thompson's honeymoon period will end. "I know it's quick, but you're starting tomorrow."

Keller smiles, spins the ball on a finger. He drops it to the floor and casually dribbles it behind his back, back and forth. "You won't be sorry," he says.

"Don't put too much pressure on yourself. Just play. Have fun."

"I'm playing, I'm having fun," Keller says.

I blow the whistle and call the team together and introduce them to Keller. "Light scrimmage today," I tell them. "No plays until we get to know each other. Nothing fancy. Just freelance and play the game."

I roll the ball out and sit in the bleachers. Keller fits in perfectly. Latimore's out on the wing, break after break, finishing like a pro. The spacing, which has been our biggest problem, falls into place. Money gets clean looks without having to run off too many screens. Keller penetrates—they roll down, he hits Money spotted up. They shut off his lane—he hits Hedda or Latimore cutting to the hole. They look like a team and they wipe the floor with the substitutes.

After practice, I run into Darnell in the parking lot.

"Can I get a ride, coach?"

"What's up?"

"Piss in a jar day," he says. "Then a meeting."

Latimore's under court-ordered NA meetings and his contract stipulates drug tests. "Sure. Hop in."

He thanks me and gets in the car and I'm reminded again that this world is not made for tall people. I'm normal person tall, but Darnell, like most power forwards and centers is circus tall. His knees are up at his chest and his shoulders are all tucked in like he's been shoved into one of those magician's disappearing boxes.

"Sorry," I say. "Seat's broken."

"I'll live."

I pull onto the street. Traffic's heavy and it's stop and go toward the hospital.

"What do you think of Keller?" I say as we stop at a light.

Darnell looks at me. "He can play a little."

"I'm thinking CBA, maybe Europe," I say.

"Could be," Darnell says. "No further with that shot. But he's a solid minor leaguer. He'll help." He takes a breath. "Is this it for the deals?"

"If I wanted to trade you, I would have," I say.

"Someone wanted me?"

I nod.

"Shit." He shakes his head. "Don't know who's crazier. Them for wanting me or you for keeping me."

The light changes and I slip the car into gear.

"You surprised there was interest?" I say.

"In me? Very."

A few minutes later, I can see the hospital up ahead.

"Almost there," I say.

"Whoopee," Darnell says. He blows an imaginary new year's noisemaker and looks out the windshield with a tired smile.

"It bother you?" I say.

He gives me a hard look and doesn't say anything for a minute. "Wouldn't matter if it did. But, yeah, being reminded twice a week that I fucked myself out of a life three times over kinda wears thin, coach."

I turn into the parking lot. "Sorry."

"Ain't your fault."

"Not sorry in a responsible sense," I say. "Just sorry in the general sense. That you have to go through it." I stop the car.

"You ever been to a meeting?" he says.

"AA, not NA."

"Same shit," he says. "Everybody wants to tell their little stories of how they fucked up and what they lost." We get out of the car and Darnell looks down at me over the top of the Toyota. "They want to make friends, you know? We're buddies, us fuck-ups."

"I never took much to it, either," I say. "Part of recovery, I guess." I feel stupid as soon as I say it.

"Never figured that out," Darnell says. "No point in my life I want back. What the hell am I'm supposed to be recovering?" He shakes his head and walks across the lot. "You'll wait?" he calls back.

"I'll wait."

"Wish me luck," he says. I look at him. "Just kidding, coach." He waves and walks toward the hospital.

25

THE HOUSE is packed. Our first sell-out. Parcell plastered it all over the papers and radio that The Sarasota Sun will be the first men's team ever to start a woman. ESPN II sends a crew and they're courtside along with the local reporters. It's a zoo. The press treats Hedda like she's a freak—which she is—and a joke—which she's not.

The team's running warm-ups. I walk over and pull her aside. "You OK?"

She nods. "Just a game."

"Just stay in control," I say. "Play within yourself."

"No problem," she says.

"It's not charity," I say. "I've got my best five starting." I start to walk back toward the sideline.

Chucky Hoops is back. Talk in the papers is that The Hawks and The Nets are looking for shooting guards. Since Petrovic died in that car accident, The Nets are thin at the two spot. The Hawks went with Augmon—who can't shoot beyond fifteen, and Ehlo—who's old and slow, last year. I wave at Chucky and he waves back. Behind our bench, Rube Parcell sits with a game program rolled up in one hand—The Chicken Man thinks he's John Wooden. I go to the bench to get some water.

"How's my coach?"

"Good," I say. "Nervous."

"All the great ones get nervous, boy. A good sign."

"Sure," I say. I look back at the team. Losers get nervous, too, I think. People that are about to get their asses kicked, they get nervous. I look over to the other bench and Clem Garret looks back and shakes his head. The paper, after the screaming incident, quoted him saying I didn't belong in coaching.

For five minutes, it's half-court ball—slow and deliberate with both teams looking to post up. Their point guard, Bill Sterrs, is a good half-court player, and he's getting the ball down low pretty well—good clean entry passes full of deception. He's a step slower than Keller, though, and he doesn't go left well. I call time, with us down 10-5.

"We're going to press," I tell the team as they sit. "1-3-1 full court. Darnell, you're on the ball. Lewie, go middle. Hedda and Money on the wings. Grant, stay back," I say and draw the little X's on my clipboard. "I want total energy—give it everything full court. You need a blow, give me a signal." I clap and get them out of the huddle. As they start toward the court, I call Lewie, Hedda and Money over.

"Sterrs can't go left without putting his head down. The minute the head goes down, I want the trap. Not before. Watch his head."

The trap kills them. We didn't run it the other night—I didn't have the right players—and it's obvious Garret didn't prepare them. We shade Sterrs right, force him left, and throw the trap. We get six steals in the quarter. Hedda gets loose on the wings, Darnell gets a couple of dunks hanging back, and Keller scores on a couple of breakaways. At the end of the quarter, we're up 35-22. The crowd is into the game, Parcell winks at me every time I look up, and I feel like a genius.

Midway through the second quarter, the game's going so well that I run out of things to say. I should just sit on the bench and enjoy, but I'm full of this nervous energy, so I keep pace the floor and scream coaching clichés. "Trap," I yell. "Hit the trailer. See the ball. Rotate, damnit, rotate."

I'm yelling to feel like I'm doing something at this point. They don't hear any of this, and they don't need to. At the half, we're up 25. My throat is sore as hell, but I'm jazzed. I forgot what winning felt like—how good it is to own the opposition. On the way into the tunnel, I pass by Chucky Hoops.

"See you after the game?" he says.

"Bad news?" I say.

"Depends on who's getting it," Chucky says.

"After the game," I say.

It's about Money—I know it. Luckily, though, pro camps don't start for a while, so no one's going to take him from me right away. I walk away from Chucky, head down, and wonder how long I'll have the team together. My three best players—Money, Darnell, and Keller—they could get a better offer anytime. Plus, Darnell is one slip away from the end of his career.

For the third quarter, none of it matters. Money hits everything he throws up. The trap still gives them fits. At a time-out, Garret walks over to me at the scorer's table.

"Call off the dogs," he says. "This one's over."

"Fuck off, Clem." I walk back to the huddle.

Hedda puts up ten in the quarter and, when I pull the other starters with two minutes left in the third, I leave her in. The crowd goes nuts every time she touches the ball. I keep her on the floor—let her have this moment. She's becoming bigger than the win, but she's earned it. We stretch the lead to 38 early in the fourth. I pull her and she gets a standing ovation. The camera crews start to come toward her when she takes a seat. The game's still going on and I walk over in front of the bench.

"Get the fuck away from my bench," I yell. I overreact, but I don't want to turn this into a circus. The camera guy looks at me. "I've got players out there," I say and point. "You'll get your interviews. Show some respect."

I feel like an asshole, like a parent, but when I look up, there's Parcell. He smiles, nods and taps his head a couple of times with the rolled-up program. "Good show, Ben Thompson," he says. He lights a victory cigar. First he's Wooden, now he's Red Auerbach.

The game enters garbage time and gets ugly with both teams running around without doing anything. We win by thirty. When I get to the locker room, Money keeps making fun of me. He drags his right leg, hunches over like Quasimodo.

"Get the fuck away from my bench," he says. "Me coach. You media."

"It was that bad?" I say.

"You are one territorial son of a bitch," Money says. He wears a towel, and zips down an imaginary fly and makes like he's pissing on the bench. "My bench," he says. "Stay away. Me in control. Me protect players."

Darnell walks by me on his way to the showers. "You're gonna have a heart attack," he says and smiles. "Losing stresses you out and winning might kill you."

"Practice tomorrow at two," I say. They nod. The locker room is fun for the first time—winning makes life easy.

I meet Chucky Hoops in my office. A couple of NBA teams and one in Europe want to get a look at Money in pre-season. Our season ends October 4—right before NBA camps start. I ask Chucky to keep it quiet and not tell Money or his agent. He's still got a lot of work to do on his game and I want him to stay desperate. He plays better without a safety net. Chucky agrees to go along with me.

26

I GO OUT on the court and ESPN II is still talking to Hedda. She's in her jersey on the bench under those interrogation lights they use for TV. She towels off her face and waves. I wave back, go out to the parking lot and head to The Bunker.

When I get there, Terry's at the bar talking to Bone and Parcell's topless cleaner.

"The big winner," Terry says as I limp to a stool. "Club sodas all around."

"One in a row isn't much of a streak."

"It's how they all start, Bomber," Terry says.

"True enough," I say. Terry puts a club soda and lime in front of me.

"You don't drink?" the topless cleaner says.

"Not don't," I say. "Can't."

"Health?"

"Something like health." I take a sip and look at her. She's got on a pair of faded and torn jeans, a black silk shirt, and a leather biker jacket. Her short red hair looks nice against the black and blue. "Why are you being nice to me, Joanna?"

She puts out her hand. Terry and Bone move down the bar a little. "Confession time. My name's Sean. Joanna's one of my professional names."

I shake her hand. "So, why is Sean being nice to me? I got the impression I wasn't one of your favorite people."

She sips her beer. "You might not be. The jury's still out." She rolls a cigarette, licks the little glue strip and lights it. "But Hedda and Bone said you were a decent human being, so I thought I'd drop by and see."

"You know Hedda and Bone?" I say, pleased that Hedda had something nice to say about me.

"Bone does most of my piercings."

"Piercings?" I say. "I didn't see any in Parcell's office."

"I take them out for work," she says. "Plus, you didn't see all of me in the office."

"Bone does your piercings," I say more to myself to let it sink in. I look over at Bone and he raises his glass, looking straight ahead.

"He introduced me to Hedda. And Mr. Parcell said I had the wrong impression of you. Thought we should meet."

"The Chicken Man's pimping me out?" I say. It was meant to be funny and charming, but it came out wrong and I feel stupid.

She shakes her head. If she's offended, she doesn't let on. "No. If you were going to get fucked tonight—which you are not—then he'd be pimping you." She drinks her beer. "Not pimping. Facilitating. You've got a lot of friends."

"Looks that way." I look over at Terry and Bone. "You getting all of this?"

"Almost," Bone says.

"Talk louder," Terry says.

She says, "I should get going."

"Really?" I say.

"I've got work to do. I just wanted to set things better between us and I wanted to talk with you. We'll have lunch. I can call you?" she says.

"You can call me," I say. "Drop by. Whatever."

She gets off her stool and puts her pouch of Drum into this metal purse she has that looks like a canteen. "You boys'll talk about me when I go, right?"

"You know it," Bone says.

She walks up the stairs. I look at Terry and Bone, then back to the empty stairwell.

"You could've looked that time, coach," she calls down. "A missed opportunity." The door opens and closes.

Terry gives me another drink. "You're having a nice day."

"No kidding." I look at him. "A perfect night."

Bone shakes his head. "Perfect would have been if she wanted dinner. Lunch isn't the best sign."

"No?" I say.

Terry nods. "Dinner would have been better. Even just drinks would've been better."

"Lunch is the least intimate of all the meals," Bone says.

"Says who?"

"Am I right?" Bone says to Terry.

Terry looks at me. "The man speaks the truth."

"Lunch is bad?" I say.

"Didn't say that," Bone says. "This is early. Lunch is better than nothing. It's just the meal with the least amount of sexual overtone. Dinner can lead to a fuck. So can drinks. Breakfast is very intimate. A private meal. Full of sex. Breakfast is personal."

"Woman invites you to breakfast, you're doing fine," Terry says.

Bone nods and taps on the bar. "But lunch. Lunch suggests nothing and leads to nothing—for the most part." He sips his beer. "Lunch offers very little."

"You can get a dinner out of lunch," Terry says.

"True," Bone says. "It can lead to a better meal. Lunch is a try-out, at best."

"Everybody knows this?" I say.

Terry shrugs. "Everybody but you, Bomber. A minor league meal."

"What do you know about her?" I say to Bone.

"Smart. Got her Ph.D. a while back. Dr. Cohen. She taught part-time at Ringling last year. Composition. She's working on a book—something about shitty jobs," he says.

"The topless cleaning?" I say, still unclear on the whole deal.

He nods. "Topless cleaner, stripper, phone sex—shit like that."

"Really?" I say. "Why?"

"She's interested in 'women's issues,'" he says, making that annoying quotation mark gesture with his middle and index fingers. People do that, they remind me of Nixon, though I don't think I ever saw him do it.

●27

IT'S ANOTHER HOT, slimy night and the mosquitoes eat me up on the way back to The Palms. The smell of chicken shit festers in the dense air. The bugs, they're relentless—little Joe Frazier bugs—and I make it home with these welts as big as pinkie knuckles all over my arms and neck.

I turn on the TV and flip through the channels. Late night crap. "American Gladiators," lame movies and the usual infomercials—the hair cutter that hooks up to your vacuum, the pasta-maker guy, the juicer guy, that shocking blonde screaming woman who lost a lot of weight. I think that's her hook. After a couple of runs through the channels, I mute the sound and keep clicking.

I stop on ESPN II—they're showing a re-run of "The World's Strongest Man" competition. I remember this. It was originally on CBS in the 70's. They'd gather all these chunky power lifters and football linemen. I turn the sound up and Brent Musburger does his best to make this sound like a legitimate sport.

They're racing up a fifty yard hill with refrigerators strapped to their backs, these fat guys are. They wear red and blue clingy outfits and look like college wrestlers. Bruce-somebody beats all the other fat red-faced huffers and puffers up the hill with his appliance. Musburger interviews him at the top of the hill.

"I saw Tony straining," Bruce says. "So I just put my head down and went on up." Two lackeys unstrap the refrigerator from his back and he springs forward.

"Good show," Musburger says. "And good luck in the Girl Lift."

He thanks Musburger and turns to the meager crowd and pumps his meaty fists into the air. The crowd, they love this guy.

They show the leader board, and Bruce is way out in front of the others.

"Barring a disaster in the final event, it looks at if he's got his second title wrapped up," Musburger says, as they go to commercial. Coming up, the screen reads, The Girl Lift.

I click through the channels quickly during the break. Every couple of minutes, the blind cow thumps against the side of the building. You can hear it up on the second floor. Bone says she's in heat—it happens every once in a while—and she runs against cars and walls and things all night. The other cows are in heat too, but they're not much of a problem. The apartment thumps twice more. Someone, I think it's Money, shouts, "I'm going to kill that fucking animal."

The competition starts again and everyone is in place for the Girl Lift. It's at a beach—I think it's Venice. You can see the ocean in the background. The fat guys all have 70's bushy hair—a couple have those silly white guy perms—that blows in the breeze. Bruce, the big leader, he's got these Fat Elvis sideburns that border on muttonchops. One by one, they go to the bar.

The bar has 150 pounds on it. There is a cage, connected through this gyroscope of metal, above them and the bar. Empty, it weights 50 pounds. It can't fall on them—there's a safety device that keeps the cage six feet from the ground. They all lift the bar and empty cage.

"Let's start adding girls," Musburger says. The crowd cheers.

Again, one by one, The Embraceable Ewes—the LA Rams cheerleaders get in the cage.

"Toni is a dancer from Pasadena," Musburger says as the woman in the cheerleader outfit climbs into the cage over the fat guy. "She's 112 pounds. Along with Karen, that brings the total to 417 pounds."

After six cheerleaders are cramped into the cage, Musburger says, "What a display of strength. How many girls can these competitors lift?"

Beneath the caged women, the fat guys wobble and change color from pasty white to blotchy red. Some lift, some don't, and it's down to Kyle-somebody—winner of the telephone poll toss—and Bruce—the refrigerator race winner.

Kyle can't lift seven cheerleaders. Bruce, who already has the title wrapped up motions the remaining two cheerleaders into the cage.

"Amazing," Musburger says. "Folks, he doesn't need to do this, but he going to lift all the girls." The crowd cheers.

Bruce gets under the caged women. He takes a couple of deep breaths, steadies himself and, after a small wobble, gets the cage up. The cheerleaders oh and ah, do a parody of surprise. Bruce bails out from under the cage and the women bounce a couple of times before the cage comes to a rest. A couple of them look a little shaken.

"What a competitor," Musburger says.

I click through the channels again. A guy sets fire to the hood of a 65 Mustang. "Easy Clean will makes it good as new," he says. The wall rattles. The blind cow moans. I change the channels. Australian Rules football—a bunch of guys beating the shit out of each other for no apparent reason. I don't understand it, and I watch, fascinated in a bored sort of way. The wall shakes and rattles again. The cow moans—a tortured and lonely sound. Parcell—dressed up as The Chicken Man—is yelling on one of the stations I click by.

"Shut the fuck up," Money—this time I'm sure it's him—screams.

I click back to the burning Mustang station. The fire's out, a woman from the audience wipes it clean. It shines, candy apple red, under the studio lights.

"Isn't that amazing?" the host says. The audience claps.

28

THE BASEBALL strike's still on, and we get a little coverage in the paper. Most of the story's about Hedda, but Darnell and Money get some ink, too. I read the paper out by the pool, which is still drained. The early morning sun warms me, and I feel mildly relaxed for the first time in years. My knee starts to stiffen up and I lie down on the ground for a while, but the sandspurs dig too much. I walk down into the deep end of the pool and stretch out on the bottom. A shadow blocks the sun.

"You OK?" Bone says, standing near the diving board, which still leans, rusted, toward the pool.

"I'm OK. Good, in fact." Bone moves a little and I have to shade my eyes with my hand. "There's a lot about Hedda in the paper."

"Read it," he says. He moves back in front of the sun and I put my hand down. "I had no idea she was that good."

"Don't base an opinion on one game," I say. He moves. "Stay still."

"Sorry." He comes down into the pool and sits against the side. He wears the same paint-smeared cut-offs he had the night we met. In addition to the nipple rings, he's got one in his belly button.

"That new?" I say and point.

He shakes his head. "Nope. Don't always wear them all." He grabs his head and pulls it toward his shoulder. His neck makes a series of cracks. "I didn't see all of the game—I meant from the article. Player of the year twice and all that. I had no idea."

I close my eyes. "She was something in college. You don't get to a pro league—even a shitty one—if you suck." I make a shooting gesture, hold the follow-through. "Everyone I've got was a star somewhere."

"Really?" He lights a cigarette.

"You watch a professional game, and you're looking at players that've been stars their whole lives—most of them, anyway. Some of the bigger guys—the seven footers—they're not much, but you need size and there just aren't that many big people around." I sit up. "Anyone under six-nine, though—you're looking at someone who knows what it feels like to be a star."

Bone looks up at The Palms and points. "This must suck for them, then."

"Everyone here's on the way up or the way down. This is not the direct route to anywhere. I've got four or five that want to go up—but only Money and Latimore have a shot. The rest—Shasky, Fillmore and Karpov—are on their way out. No one wants to be in The Gulf Coast League. Except Hedda. She's the only one this could be a success for. Already is—she's a first." I flip over and take my shirt off, the sun heats my back. "You should go congratulate her. She did something special last night."

"I don't want to bother her," he says. He takes a drag of his cigarette. "You think she likes me, Ben?"

I turn my head and look at him. "I don't know. I'm just her coach." He seems disappointed. "She's letting you do her tattoo."

He shrugs. "I do a lot of them. I'm good. Doesn't mean anything."

"I thought it might." I roll over.

"It could," he says. "But it doesn't have to."

"I thought maybe it was a good sign—trust wise."

He gets up. "It might be." He does a pull-up out of the pool. "Time to get to work. Take it easy, Ben."

I wave and roll back onto my stomach. I spend most of the morning trying to get some extra sleep. Around ten, the team, one by one, starts waking up and my privacy is ruined. I head to my room and take a shower.

29

WE TAKE the first three games of a four game road trip. We fly to Galveston and kick the shit out of The Galveston Rangers 123-96. The gym was empty—you could have counted the fans—and talk is that the Rangers might fold before the season ends, and cut the league down to seven teams. From Galveston, we take a chartered bus to New Orleans where we beat The Bayou Dogs by twenty. Two days later, we head up the road to Mississippi and take a close one from The Jackson Gators. Latimore's Achilles was sore and I rested him most of the second and third quarters. Money and Keller came up big, though, and we did enough to win. I pulled

Money in the third quarter and screamed at him for not playing D. Two or three minutes of the game went by with me in his face yelling. I put him back in the fourth and he won the game for us.

After midnight, we're on the bus again, headed east on 20 to play The Montgomery Rebels tomorrow night. I take a seat up front, look at the Rebels roster, and listen to the tires hiss on the road. Money comes up behind me.

I hand him the roster. "You know any of these guys?"

He takes it and looks down the list. "Personally, or game?"

"Either. But I'm more concerned with their games."

"Daniel Jefferson," he says and taps the clipboard. "Slasher. Aggressive."

"He got size?" I say.

He shakes his head. "Undersized three. Quick. He's thin, though. Hedda could post him, but he could give her trouble on the other end. No jumper, but he's relentless going to the hole." He hands the roster back to me. "The rest of these are just names."

"The first time we play them, they're just names. Next week, when we get them at home, I want you to be able to write a book about—" I check their shooting guard's name on the roster—"Derrick Hancock. His moves, his tendencies, his whole game. I quiz you, and you'll tell me his height, weight, strengths, weaknesses, and what he likes for dinner."

He looks down at me for a moment, and slides into the seat. He leans toward me. "Why the fuck you dog me like this?"

"I'm dogging you?"

"What do you call it?"

I shake my head. "Coaching you." I take a deep breath. "You want to get out of this league?"

He points at the Montgomery roster. "I don't belong with those names." He slaps the clipboard with the back of his hand. "You know that."

"You know who Les Harding is?"

He rolls his eyes. "No."

"Les Harding played one minute for Miami back in '92. Look up his stat line. One minute—no points, no rebounds, no assists—not even a fucking foul. Nothing."

"It's my fault I never heard of this guy?"

"He was better than you."

"Bullshit. Some one-minute nothing better than me? He's nobody."

"He made it. That minute put him in the record books. You can look up Les Harding." I point at my chest. "You can't look up Ben Thompson." I point at him. "And you can't look up Kenny Cash—no matter how pretty his game might be. You know how many guys with pretty games ended up nowhere? I know nothing about this guy and I'd trade places with him. He could have the most miserable existence on this planet—be dirt poor and have tumors on his balls—and I'd trade. That's how much you should want it. You think I'm dogging you, that's fine. But if you listen to me, someone might be able to find you in that book someday, and you might stick for a little longer than a minute."

He sits quietly for a moment and takes the roster from me, looks, and gives it back. "I put this Hancock chump in my pocket, and you leave me alone?"

"No. This isn't a one-shot deal. I'll leave you alone when you get the call. Your game's full of holes. I don't tell you that to hurt your feelings—it's the truth and someone before me should have done it."

"Well, thank you, Kenny Cash's savior." His voice is cold and angry. He shakes his head and gets up. "Can't fucking win here." I hear him grumbling his way through the bus. It's under his breath, but he wants me to hear him. "Sarasota Shit. Sarasota Headache. Sarasota fucking pain in my ass." He sits a few seats behind me. "You watch your boy Hancock tomorrow, coach," he calls above the seats. "See what's left of him when I'm done."

Lights zip by the other way on the dark road. I wonder if I was a little hard on him—he's worked a lot on his game since he's been here and he's close, real close, to where he should be. Around two, the rhythm of the bus rumbling over the wet pavement puts me to sleep.

 30

"**M**ONTGOMERY REBELS," Darnell says. It's two minutes to tip-off and he comes over by the bench to get some water. He shakes his head.

"What?" I say.

"Their name. Rebels." He crushes the little triangular paper cup and tosses it behind the bench. "Makes you wonder if these crackers are ever gonna know they were on the wrong side of that war." He looks at me. "You don't find their name problematic, politically speaking?"

"I didn't," I say. "But I do. Hadn't thought about it."

He raises his eyebrows and smiles, but it's a mean smile that says I'm not so bright. "Not something you have to think about, is it?" He pats me on the shoulder and sits on the bench. The horn blows and the team comes to the sideline.

Kenny Cash hasn't talked to me since our conversation on the bus. He's got a stern game face on—eyes that look through things, and not at them. He's either mad as hell or focused beyond belief. Maybe both.

The game starts and it becomes apparent that this Hancock is the focus of their offense. They isolate him and John Gale—a big, slow center—on the right in a two-man game. Hancock dribbles out front and looks to Gale in the post, but Jefferson beats Hedda on a back cut. Hancock throws a one-handed pass off the dribble, hits Jefferson in stride and they're up 2-0.

"Hedda," I scream. "See the god-damn ball!"

They run the two-man game for most of the first quarter and we trade baskets. After a time-out with two minutes left in the first, Money turns to me as he heads onto the court.

"Say goodnight to Mr. Hancock," he says. "Money's got him measured." He wipes off his face and flicks the towel toward me. "Be watching."

They give the ball to Hancock at half-court and run three players weak side, the same way they've been doing it all night. Hancock dribbles out high. Money's deep in his stance, hands down, eyes riveted. He pokes the ball away and gets loose for a dunk. He runs back toward half court and looks over at me. He mouths, "one" and holds his index finger in the air.

The next time Hancock gets the ball on the wing, Money picks his pocket again. Another dunk. He runs up court and looks over at me with two fingers up.

Early in the second quarter, they try to run the two-man game again. Hancock dribbles about twenty feet from the hole. Money strips him again and starts to head toward the hoop. Hancock chases after him. At the foul line, Money stops. Hancock runs by and gets in front of him. Money hands him the ball and gets down in his defensive stance. It's the most arrogant, demeaning play I've ever seen. Money just told Hancock that he can take it from him every time, and he told him in front of two thousand people and both teams.

Rather than try to beat Money off the dribble, Hancock passes off and lets their point bring it up. After that, Hancock doesn't look for the ball on offense and Money tears him up at the other end. Everyone plays sharp, except for Darnell and we win going away. Money's still not talking to me in the locker room. I feel bad, but he played his best game. Still, it's a hell of a way to get what I want from him.

I congratulate the team and walk toward the little office cubicle. On the way, I see Darnell limping toward the trainer's table.

"Achilles?"

He nods. "And the knees."

"Put some ice on them," I say. "Tomorrow's a day off, but if you need more than that, let me know." I'm worried—he's had no major injuries, but he's got too many miles on those legs.

He takes a step away from me and winces when he puts pressure on the left leg. "Thanks. Can't afford too many days off, though."

"Get it ready for the game. Don't worry about practice."

He heads into the trainer's room and I turn around and see Money who's heard the conversation. He looks hard at me and points at the office.

I close the door behind us.

"I was all over your boy tonight," he says.

"He's not my boy," I say. "You've got this wrong."

He's already showered and dressed. Sweat still breaks on his head below the hairline and trickles down his face. "Owned him. I was inside that chump. They're going to cut Hancock up at the morgue someday, and 'Kenny Cash Was Here' is gonna be stamped on everything they see."

"You played a great game," I say.

He nods and puts his hand on the doorknob. "Nice to hear you say it."

"Don't leave," I say. "Sit. I need to tell you something." He sits and I tell him about The Hawks and Nets and the European team whose name I can't pronounce. He sits there, nodding and looking straight ahead.

"And you've known this a while?"

"About a week."

"How long were you going to hold off from telling me?"

It's a good question. "I'm not sure," I say. "Until I saw some improvement. Until I thought you were close to being ready."

"And I'm close?"

"You are. Do what you did tonight a few more times—except for that stunt with the steal—and you won't have me to deal with me anymore."

"What was wrong with the steal? I put him away with that."

"Nothing was wrong here," I say. "But you try to pull that arrogant shit at the next level and you'll have your head handed to you. Pull that attitude on Mitch Richmond or John Starks and you'll see how foolish it is."

"It worked tonight," he says.

"It did."

He smiles, but it's not a nice we've-reached-common-ground-smile. "Hypothetical. A scout's looking at D," he says and points toward the training room where Darnell is icing his knees and ankle. "Do you tell him?"

"Probably," I say.

He stops smiling. "Twenty-seven teams in the NBA—with expansion next year we're at twenty-nine. Twelve spots per team—that's 348 jobs. I've done the fucking math. Every night, every day, I do the math. 348 slots. Don't mean shit that me and D play different positions—a job for him could mean no job for me and you're willing to tell him about one of those slots, and you're not going to tell me?" He shakes his head. "Shit ain't right."

"A job for Darnell means no job for you? That's an ugly way to look at this situation," I say.

"It's a practical way to look at it. And you're dealing us different hands." He gets up. "How come you treat me and D so different?"

"I'm not sure," I say. "You're different people."

"And my reward for this is getting shit on." He opens the door and starts to leave.

"Kenny," I say. He stops and turns. "You played a hell of a game tonight. You're a player."

He looks at me a little less hard than before. "You're right," he says. "I did and I am." He closes the door and heads out toward the team bus, waiting in the parking lot. I gather my things. Most of the players are on the bus. Darnell is having trouble getting his pants on. I know that feeling—the knee won't bend enough so you throw the pants on the floor and kind of shimmy your way into them. Lewie Keller's on the phone, talking to his wife.

"Back in Sarasota tomorrow. No more pancake houses for a while," he says. "Long night." He nods. "Put her on." He turns to me with his hand over the receiver and asks if we've got tomorrow off. I tell him we do and he turns back to the payphone. "How's my little girl?"

I start to leave.

"We won. That's right, they haven't lost since they got daddy. I've got to go, honey so put your mother back on. I'll be home tomorrow. I promise."

I leave the room and get on the bus. We wait about five minutes and finally I go back to get them. When I get to the gym door, they both come out.

"Sorry coach," Lewie says. "Hard to get her off. She misses her dad."

"Don't sweat it," I say.

He runs up ahead of us and onto the bus. I look at Darnell. "You OK?"

He limps forward. "Nope. I'm old."

"You're twenty-eight. You're young," I say, trying to lighten him up. "I'm old."

"I'm as old as I've ever been," he says. "Feels old to me."

I watch him get on the bus—he lifts his body with his arms and pulls himself up—thinking, he is twenty-eight and he is old.

31

WE GET to The Palms early in the morning. The team is quiet and groggy and people head to their rooms without talking much. Keller goes home to a little apartment he's got down off twelfth street, just outside of the Mennonite community. There are no messages on my bulletin board. I check my machine in hopes that Sean might have called. Nothing except a message from The Chicken Man.

"A 4-0 road trip, Ben Thompson. Good show. Call me when you get in."

I decide to get some rest and call him later. I flop down on the bed and turn on the TV. Nothing's on but those chatty, perky morning shows full of fluff. Julia Roberts plugs some new movie. She says it's better than "Pretty Woman"—she says this like that would be a difficult thing. But people love these shows—love those movies. I shake my head, decide I don't understand much about the world and that it's probably my fault and not the world's. I turn it off, roll over and try to get some sleep.

32

LATE IN THE afternoon—still no word from Sean—I head up to Tampa for a meeting with The Chicken Man. I sit out in his office for a while and wait. Two men leave his office and the receptionist buzzes me through.

"How's my winner?" he says.

"Your winner's tired."

He gets up and walks toward the bar. He gets himself a drink and hands me a mineral water with a lime wedge in the rim. I push the lime down into the bottle and take a drink. He moves back behind his desk.

"You, Ben Thompson, wake up with a four letter word."

"Come again."

"You, like most people wake up with a four letter word—you don't know how to take on a day. I wake up with a three letter word—PEP." He holds out his hand and counts the letters off on his fingers. "P-Positive. E-Energy. And P-Program. You got to have a program. PEP."

I look at him and down at the bottle in my hand. "I'm not a PEP kind of guy," I say.

"Ben Thompson living on a chicken farm, driving some shitbox car, telling Rube Parcell he doesn't know how to start a day." He laughs a grumpy I'm-better-than-you-and-you-know-it laugh.

"Score one for you," I say.

"So, what's your program?"

I sit quietly for a moment, wondering whether I should talk with Parcell or not. "Can we talk seriously?" I say.

"I'm always serious, even when I'm joking," he says. "Serious as cancer—is cancer serious enough for you?"

"It is."

"Shoot, Ben Thompson."

I fill him in on the situation with Money and the scouts. The whole bit about Money being pissed because I treat him and Darnell differently.

"I don't see your problem," Parcell says. "You've got my team winning, you've got my players playing."

"He hates me," I say.

"Who?"

"Kenny Cash," I say. "He can't stand me."

Parcell leans forward and I see a wavy reflection of his face in the polished desk. "Why didn't you tell Cash he was being scouted?"

"To help his game," I say.

"Then you did the right thing."

"I don't think so," I say. "I've been thinking about what Money said, and he's got a point. If someone wanted Darnell, I'd tell him—Money deserves the same treatment. I didn't do right by him."

"Wrong, wrong, wrong. So very wrong it hurts me to hear you say it. You've got that young man playing better than he's ever played, right?"

I nod.

"That's doing right by him. Take whatever sense of fairness you have and throw it out a window. Being a leader, Ben Thompson, is not about being good. It's not about being kind, and it sure as hell isn't a democracy. Fuck fair. Fuck good. You think I got to this chair worrying about people's feelings? You worry about his feelings, you're fucking up. Why should you give one iota of a rat's ass what Kenny Cash thinks of you?"

I shrug. "I just do. I like him—he's a hot dog, but he's not a bad kid."

"Fine. Like him. That's your right. But your job is not to be liked—it's to win."

"I'd like to do both," I say.

"Wrong again. Can't be done." He lights a cigar and looks at the ceiling. "I haven't asked you—ever—what you thought of me, have I?"

"No," I say.

He smiles that same warm smile he gave me the first day I was here. "I like you, Ben Thompson. I liked you when I hired you and I like you more now. But I could give a shit what you think about me. I'm sure there are things about me that bother you, and that's fine. You cannot be in a position of power and be concerned about feelings. Those are diametrically opposed patterns of thought. I get concerned about you and I'm not in charge. You follow?"

"I do," I say. "I don't agree, though."

"You think you know better, and that's fine. I'm trying to give you a life lesson here, but it's your right to find out the hard way. You get Kenny Cash to like you—you work real hard on that—and I'll be sure he gets a job at a meat packing plant. You work on coaching him, and he might play in the NBA. I understand. I'm sure he'll be happier up to his elbows in pig guts, knowing that Ben Thompson is his friend."

I stand up. "Are we done?"

He motions me to sit. "We are not." He has this look of concern on his face. "You need to listen to me, Ben Thompson. You need to grow up."

"Not caring what people think of you is growing up?" I say.

"Who the hell said you shouldn't care what people think of you?" he says. "I said you shouldn't care what employees think of you. There's a difference." He leans back. "Stay on track, Ben. Ride that young man as hard as you need to. Make him hate you and don't care about how he feels. Forget he's human if that's what it takes for you to make him better. Do your job."

33

I'M IN MY ROOM, lying down, my hands behind my head. I can hear the click, click, click of the second hand of my watch. I've never known what to do with a day off. I stay by myself in a room alone too long and all I think of is the sweep of that second hand, reminding me of another wasted second after another wasted second. Death and stagnation.

I get up and decide to go to the practice courts, thinking that maybe doing something will get me out of this funk. I leave a note about where I am on my memo board in case anyone needs me.

The gym is empty except for me and some kid who's running the bleachers. The ball echoes with every dribble and the bleachers rattle with every step the kid takes. I shoot one off glass from about fifteen feet out and it falls. I run through some shooting drills—spot up going left—spot up going right. After a few minutes, I step up to the line and shoot some free throws. The kid still runs the bleachers, but after a while I don't hear it so much. Three dribbles, focus on the rim, follow through, keep the eyes on the rim. I drop ten, fifteen, twenty five in a row. Three dribbles, pause, swish.

I can't miss. It's been years since I had this feeling. Just you, the ball and the rim. Nothing else exists in the world—it's like those pictures of the Earth from outer space, only there's you and a hoop and nothing else. I stop counting and just focus on the rhythm. I've got the touch and start shooting threes. The floor shines like a bowling alley, the bleachers rock and creak under the kid's feet, and everything I throw up falls in like it had eyes.

I jab-step in and shoot a step-back fade-away from twenty. The form's good, but my legs aren't under me and it falls short with a dead clang off the rim.

"You miss."

I turn and see Sean sitting on the bleachers by the side of the court.

"I do," I say. I run and get the ball and shoot one off glass. "How long have you been here?"

"Ten, fifteen minutes," she says. "You're good."

I walk over to her. "I used to be."

"But not anymore?"

"Nope," I say and point to my knee.

Sean looks closely at the knee and runs a finger down the thickest of the scars on both sides. The scars are numb—all the nerves were severed—and I can only feel the pressure around where she's touching, not on the spot itself. "They're beautiful."

"Really?" I say.

She's wearing black jeans with a black suede vest that shows off her arms, which are more cut than mine. Black cowboy boots. It's 95 degrees out. "Is that a statement? All the black?"

She smiles. "It's a color."

"But it's not," I say.

"It's not, but it is," she says. "How about lunch?"

I'd love to have lunch with her alone, but I still have work to do before tomorrow's practice. "I'm watching some game tape at Terry's. You're welcome to come."

She thinks about it for a moment. "You and Terry and shop talk?" she says.

"Sorry," I say. "Today's kind of tight."

"Don't be sorry," she says. "Sounds like fun."

 34

WE'RE EARLY IN the second quarter of the Montgomery game. On the tape, Money steals the ball from Hancock and gives it back. Terry rewinds the play and watches it again.

"Shit," he says.

He rewinds it and plays it back again.

He shakes his head and laughs. "Wow. That's cold." He lets the tape run. "He might make it up."

"I think so," I say.

"Up?" Sean says.

"The NBA," I say. "He's leading the Gulf Coast in scoring. He's becoming a defender. He's getting there."

"He's got the meanness," Terry says. "Too much of a hot dog, but he's mean."

"He has to be mean to make it?" Sean says.

Terry pours himself a cup of coffee. "There's two ways to play the game—Keller, the little point, he's all enthusiasm and love for the game. You can see it in him, he's got that Isaiah Thomas, Earvin Johnson quality. Happy as a kid when he's on the floor."

"Magic," I say. "Magic Johnson."

"Earl Monroe was Magic when little Earvin was in diapers. Johnson could play, but you don't go giving away Monroe's nickname." He takes a sip of coffee. "Giving away someone's nickname is forgetting history. Forgetting the man who changed the game. That's like forgetting Charlie Parker and calling some kid Bird. Don't matter how good the kid is—it shouldn't be done." He gives me a look. "This is more important than you think it is, Bomber."

"What's the other way to play the game?" Sean says.

"More common. Disdain. Hatred and a lack of respect. Treat the other man like he doesn't belong on the same planet as you." He points at the screen. "That's how young Mr. Cash plays. Like if you get in his way, he'll hurt you, so you might as well get out of his way."

"How'd he play?" she says and points at me.

"All hate and anger. Like the devil on roller-skates. You know that feeling when you're leaning back in your chair, and it feels like it might topple backwards? That moment you don't know if you can get control or not where everything's up in the air?"

She nods.

"Then you know what coaching him was like," he says and gestures toward me with his mug. "When he came to us, he was so undisciplined, it was frightening. A win was a win, a loss was the end of the world. Boy would rip apart a locker room after a loss. But he had it—that meanness. Bomber took every loss personally. Still does."

"That true?" Sean says.

"I was an asshole," I say, and think about college—most everyone I played with couldn't stand me. If someone wasn't as good as me, I figured they weren't working. I yelled at my teammates, the refs, my coaches, and I trash-talked my man all night long. The me that comes out when I need to win is someone I hate.

"We were playing some division two school," Terry says. "And this kid—I forget his name."

"Leon Garriss," I say. "Don't tell this story."

"Leon Garriss is shooting off in the papers about how he's going to shut Bomber down. Ben had just hit for 42 against Georgia, and this Garriss kid says 'No way Thompson comes in our house and gets 40,' or some shit like that. So two, three days before the game, Bomber's collecting papers—he's cutting out articles and making a scrapbook. We go to the game and he's got his little leather bound book full of articles about what Garriss is going to do to Ben Thompson. Takes it to the locker room. Gets out on the floor and starts jawing with this kid—quoting him. After his first few jumpers fall, he's screaming at this Garriss kid 'No way Thompson hits for 40—not in our house.'" Terry laughs.

"Stop," I say.

Sean shushes me with her finger.

"Near half-time, Bomber's got twenty-twenty-five, and their coach screams 'Who's got him?' and Bomber's yelling at the kid, 'Who's got me?' Late in the second half, we're up twenty, and he's got?" Terry looks at me.

"47," I say.

"47. And we pull him out. The game's over, he's got a career high—he should be happy, right? He glares at this Garriss kid all the way off the court, tells him the coaches took pity on him, or he would have lit him for fifty. After the game, he autographs his little scrapbook and gives it to a reporter and tells him to give it to Garriss."

I look down at the bar, see the condensation rings from my bottle turning the bar wood a milky white. I think that Leon Garriss—wherever he is in the world—probably still thinks I'm a childish jerk. Based on what I did, he's right. "I wasn't always like that," I say. I take a drink. "Finish the story. Tell her what you did."

Terry shrugs. "We benched him for the next game. I told him it was a classless display and it was his worst game of the year."

"Both of which were true," I say. "I had 47, but I took thirty-five shots to get it. We should have beaten them by fifty. That game still bothers me. I've thought about writing Garriss a letter for years. Write it my head sometimes when I'm driving or when I can't sleep."

"Listen to you," Sean says. "Talking about a game—a game you won—fifteen years ago. You think that guy ever remembers you?"

"I'd remember me if I were him," I say. I think again of sending him that letter I should—but know I never will—write.

35

SEAN AND I go to dinner at some seafood place out on Turtle Bay. We get an outdoor table. There's a nice breeze off the bay and the air is thick with the smell of those candles they use to keep the bugs away.

"How do you like coaching?" she says.

"Is this the getting to know each other part of the day?"

"It was a question. You're new to it, right?"

"Yeah. Tell the truth, I don't know if I like it or not. Too many egos—too many people to be concerned about." I tell her some of the

Money/Darnell situation. Fill her in on the problems with Hedda that I had early in the season. "It seems like someone's always pissed at me," I say. "Hard to deal with."

"It's natural," she says. "You've got a lot of say in their lives."

"That's the problem," I say. "It's been ten years since anyone gave a shit about what I thought. I'd show up at a job, talk about the weather, the color scheme, paint for eight hours and go home and drink until I fell asleep. What I did or didn't do had no effect on people."

Sean frowns, looks down at the table.

"What?" I say.

"Weren't you married?" she says. "During this time your actions had no effect on people?"

"I was a mess—it wasn't all drinking. I just wasn't a very good person. Linda gave up on expecting anything from me a long time before we signed papers." I look out at the water. Big mouthed birds—maybe they're pelicans—skid above the water's surface and dive in every couple of minutes. "But you're right. It's just different now—a direct cause and effect." I look at her. "I screw up with Kenny Cash, I could stall his career. When you're twenty-five in basketball, a year is a lifetime. He gets one, maybe two, more shots at the big-time."

"But he's doing well," she says.

"He is. For now. It's so delicate. He needs everything to fall into place. Be at the right spot at the right time. Let's say Orlando invites him for a fall try-out. They're deep at shooting guard—if they take him he's their fifth guard—nothing but an insurance policy. He gets no chance to develop—no playing time. In two years, his career's over. No one wants a twenty-seven year-old guy whose game still needs polish. And Darnell scares the hell out of me. I think he needs someone to push him—force him to be the player he was."

She eats a shrimp, adds another skin to the pile on the paper plate between us. "So why don't you?"

I shake my head. "Can't. Every time I feel like I should push him, I'll pull back. Every time Darnell's been close in his career, he's fucked up. Pressure destroys him." I look back at the water. Some clouds go over us and it's cold for a moment and then warm again as they pass. "I don't want to be the one responsible for pushing him back to coke." I shake my head. "The whole deal's brought back my ulcer. I don't sleep too well—I'm always on edge."

"So quit," she says.

I laugh. "I can't. I think I might love it." I look at her. She leans forward to eat over her plate and I try to see if I can spot her nipple ring. She looks up and catches me. She smiles and pulls back her vest, exposing her right breast. There's a silver hoop with a black ball in her nipple. She puts the vest back. I look away, and then at the other tables to see if anyone noticed.

"Prude," she says. "I know you. You won't ask me anything that's on your mind, but you'll go back and ask Terry or Bone what they think about me. Right?"

"You got me," I say.

"Don't blow your chance," she says. "Ask."

"Bone told me you were working on a book?"

"Which is what you say, but what you mean is 'why do you work in the sex industry?'"

"OK. Why topless cleaning.?"

"After I finished my dissertation, I went on the job market. There are very few jobs in English, and even fewer in Post-Structuralist Feminism. I needed money, and I got sick of five bucks an hour temping and the slave wages you get for teaching little Rush Limbaugh clones composition. I took a job dancing at a club."

"A club?"

"Strip bar," she says. "But I didn't strip—I didn't know how yet. I was a cage dancer."

"I've always had a weakness for cage dancers."

"How could you not?" she says. "Anyway, I got treated better at the club then I was ever treated as a secretary. Which was interesting—I was, in a way, more of a piece of meat when I was a word processor than when I was a piece of meat. And the money was good. I moved on to stripping—the money was better. I found the power dynamic interesting, so I started trying other jobs. Now I'm doing the cleaning once a week, and phone sex the rest of the time. The idea for the book just kind of grew out of all that."

"I'm still a little unclear on the book."

"It's pretty complex. About gender roles and power. Obviously, it has to address economy. The power of the erotic. Ritual and anonymity. I'll show you some of it if you want."

"Sure," I say. "Do you like the jobs?"

She looks out at the water and then back to me. "That's not a yes or no question. Some of it's very interesting. Some of it's arousing and some of it's depressing. I'll give the whole story some time, but I don't want to go into it. The phone sex is probably the best of it. I get to talk dirty, which is fun, I get paid, and I get people being honest—which is a very rare thing." She takes a drink.

"Honest? Don't people lie all the time on the phone?"

"It's a different kind of honest. They're honest about their desire—not their job or their height or weight. It's a more important honesty," she says. "What turns you on, Ben?"

I look down at the table.

"See?" she says. "You can't be honest about desire. You're worried I'll think you're a freak, right?"

"I don't know if freak's the right word—it's just a hard question to answer."

"It shouldn't be," she says. "But it's not in the script, it's not what you talk about over dinner. This culture's very interesting about sex." She reaches into her metal purse. As she opens the top, it catches the sun like a flashbulb for a second. She writes a number on a post-it note and hands it to me. Under the number is the name Cassandra.

"Call me," she says. "You tell me what turns you on. I'll tell you. We'll trade stories."

"Really?"

"It'll be fun," she says. "You'll see."

"I don't know," I say.

"What if I said I wouldn't sleep with you until you do this for me?"

"That could tip the scales," I say.

⚬36

I GET BACK to The Palms about sunset. Bone's lifting weights out by his storage garage. The weights, he's painted them all bright colors—the fives are yellow, the tens are neon blue, the fifteens are Cadillac pink. He's doing alternate curls when I walk up to him.

"All this athleticism has inspired me," he says. He's lean—a good body, if a little thin.

"You ever played ball?" I say.

"Basketball?"

"No foosball. Of course basketball," I say. "Darnell's sore as hell. If he can't go, I've only got nine players. I need a warm body for a scrimmage tomorrow. You interested?"

He does a couple more curls, one right, one left. "Can't," he says and grunts with the weights. "Heart murmur."

"Really? A bad one?"

"Not that bad, but bad enough. Can't take the risk. Sorry, Ben"

"No problem. I thought you might enjoy it." He puts the yellow weights down and starts working his triceps with the pink ones. "Sorry," I say. "I didn't know."

He stands up. "Not you fault." He bends down over the bench and starts on the left arm. "Me and Hedda are going to see Citizen Kane at the art house tonight. You want to come?"

"You don't want to be alone?"

"Not yet," he says. "I'd appreciate it if you came along."

I think about calling Sean, but we've spent a lot of time together today, and I don't want to wear thin on her. "Cool if we ask Terry?" I say.

"Go for it," he says. "Meet you at the pool at nine?"

I nod and head up to my room.

37

A T QUARTER TO NINE, I head over to The Bunker and ask Terry if he's got any plans for the night.

"I'm running a business here," he says.

I look around. He and I are the only people here. "You close whenever you want."

"True enough," he says. "What's up?"

"Me, Hedda and Bone are going to see Citizen Kane at the art house. Interested?"

He shakes his head and wipes down the bar. "Seen it."

"You can see a great movie more then once."

"True. But that ain't no great movie," he says. "White man's tragedy." He shakes his head again. "Got no time for that."

"That's ridiculous."

"No it's not. Some rich white man comes close to owning half the world and the he loses it. Then he says 'Rosebud' and people go fucking nuts trying to figure it out." Terry opens his eyes wide and puts his hands up on his cheeks and does a mocking imitation of surprise. "And it turns out it was his sled when he was a poor little boy." He smiles. "Man has to own half of everything and live to be sixty to discover that the world ain't his particular oyster? A very white thing to do. Black folks are born with that little tidbit of information—don't need to live to be sixty to figure it out."

"I don't think the world's my oyster," I say.

"No. But I'm talking general here."

I lean over the bar and pour myself some water.

"It's not that simple," I say. "The movie."

"No, it's not. But it does two things I got no patience for. It romanticizes poverty and it's nostalgic. Poverty is poverty and nostalgia is white."

"No black Rosebuds?" I say.

"No black Rosebuds."

"I never though of it that way," I say. I finish my water. "So you don't want to come?"

"No. I appreciate the offer, though." He turns on the TV. "Stop by after."

"You got it." I head up the stairs and over to The Palms.

38

BONE AND HEDDA are by the pool.

"No Terry?" Hedda says.

I shake my head. "Just us. He wants us to stop by after, though."

"No can do," Bone says. "I've got a job later."

"At night?" I say.

We start to walk to Bone's truck. "He's doing tattoos at Show Folks," Hedda says.

"Which is what?"

I hold the passenger door for Hedda. They both stop and look at me.

"You're serious?" Bone says. "You've never heard of Show Folks?"

"This is a crime?"

"It's the circus bar," Hedda says. "All the freaks drink there."

"Lobster Boy drank there," Bone says.

Sarasota was the winter home for the circuses. That, I knew, but I hadn't made any connection. "Lobster Boy?"

Bone pulls out of the driveway. The truck is suffocating and I roll down the window. "You been living in a cave, Ben?" Bone says. "Lobster Boy. He had this hand problem."

"Disease," Hedda says.

"A disease is a problem," Bone says. "Anyway, he had these fat, chunky claws for hands." He takes his hands off the wheel and makes awkward lobster claw gestures that make him look like a fifties sci-fi robot. The truck swerves. He grabs the wheel and rights it. "He married some normal woman—they had kids—I don't think the kids had lobsteritis, but I'm not sure. Apparently he was a bastard. Drank a lot, beat the shit out of her with his claws. They split up and she married some circus midget."

"This is true?" I say. He turns the truck out onto 41.

"Everybody knows about Lobster Boy," Hedda says.

Bone says, "All true. Things don't work out between her and the midget and she remarries Lobster Boy. Still beats her. Drunk all the time. Smokes Luckies by the carton."

"And?" I say.

"Blew his head off with a shotgun. They found him on the couch, a carton of smokes and a bottle of whisky on a TV tray in front of him. Don't know how he squeezed the trigger. That's all I know," Bone says. "If I find out more tonight, I'll fill you in."

"How many of them are left? There isn't a circus anymore, is there?"

"Not like the old circus. But a lot of the old-timers still live here. Freaks have to retire, too, you know."

"You're doing tattoos for retired circus people," I say. "Strange world."

He nods. "A couple small originals and one cover-up."

"How'd you get this gig?"

"Word of mouth," he says.

Citizen Kane is pretty much like I remembered it, but it has a new lens. I sit there, thinking about what Terry said and he's right—it seems sometimes like everybody I know has a better fix on life, a clearer picture, than me. I could live to be a hundred and be wrong about everything. Kane's not that sad a movie. It's still beautiful to look at, but I find myself drifting, playing out scenes of despair and violence. The Lobster Boy beating his wife with those pathetic claws. Living in some trailer, chain-smoking over a TV tray. Stained carpets and sad dull-eyed kids. And I'm watching Kane and his first wife eating dinner farther and farther apart—that scene where they keep eating at a bigger and bigger table—and thinking: so what?

About half-way through the movie, I start to think of different ways to swing the ball when they double-team Darnell in the post. It gives me something to do, and I feel better.

After the movie, Bone drives me back to The Palms. He grabs his tattoo gun and he and Hedda head off to the circus bar.

39

I WAVE TO Terry when I get down to the bottom of the stairs. There are a couple of customers at the bar. Billy, the last of the six-string outlaws, drinks in the back, next to the pool tables. He has his guitar with him, but, thankfully, he's not playing.

Terry says, "Got your friend over there. You want to ask him about his urological surgery?"

"Not really." I sit. Terry gives me a club soda. "Coffee, too." He turn and pours and places it in front of me. "You ruined the movie for me."

"One man's opinion, Bomber." He raises his hands in a what-me? gesture. "Sorry to burst your bubble."

"I'll live," I say and sip my coffee. "You ever heard of Lobster Boy?"

"Of course."

"I hadn't. Never heard of the guy, and then I find out he's famous." I shake my head. "You ever feel really out of touch with the world?"

"Every day," he says. "What are you getting at?"

"You know, like you read in the paper that some song's been number one for 10 weeks or some movie's set all kinds of records. And you've never heard of them. I don't mean never heard the song or seen the movie, I'm talking never even knew they existed, when the rest of the world is nuts for them." I rap on the bar with the back of my hand a couple of times. "It's like I took ten years off from everything, and now I don't know anything. Like I missed class, and everyone's ahead of me."

"You got all this from Lobster Boy?"

"It's just an example. I feel slow when I'm around Parcell, Sean, you—even Bone. Everyone seems to know more than me—probably even Billy," I say and point to the six-string outlaw who's asleep in his chair.

Terry frowns in thought. "Hoops. You know the game."

"Not as well as you."

"I disagree, but thanks. You're where you belong, Bomber. You can coach."

I take a deep breath. "Maybe, but I could use some help." I look up at him. "What do you say?"

"To what?"

"You want to coach with me?"

He shakes his head.

"You won't think about it?" I say.

"Don't need to," he says. "Have thought about it—don't want any part of it anymore."

"You're a great coach," I say. "I know."

"A matter of debate, but you might be right." He pours himself another cup of coffee. "Took me till I was forty to realize that just cause you can do something don't mean you should do it."

"You'd relate to the players better than me," I say.

"Because I'm black?"

"Partially. There are areas of common ground I don't have with most of my players. Plus, you played pro. That carries weight I don't have."

He looks down at the bar and doesn't say anything.

"We can't talk about this?" I say.

"We are talking about this," he says. "You just don't like the results."

I look behind Terry to the wall of bottles. There's a mirror behind them, and I see myself, fragmented between all those pretty colors. "Why?" I say. I move back and forth and watch as I swell and shrink in the warped reflection. It's like a fun house mirror.

"I can't do it, Bomber. It ate me up."

I stop moving and look at him. "It doesn't have to. Plus, this isn't college—there's less corruption."

"Corruption doesn't have degrees." He rubs his forehead with his palm. "You really want to have this discussion?"

"I do."

"You know Len Bias, right? You know we recruited him?"

"Who didn't?"

"OK. He ends up at Maryland, playing for Lefty Drissell. Everyone says what a great kid he is, pulling a B-average in his classes, drafted second overall for the Celtics. Going to take over for Bird and carry the torch."

"And drops dead of a cocaine OD the next night," I say. "Everyone knows Bias."

Terry nods. "So he's dead and all of the sudden, we find out the young man didn't have a 3.0 in his senior year, but a shitty GPA, and he hadn't finished his Sophomore year of classes, let alone Junior and Senior. Turns out it wasn't the first time he'd tried blow, like they first said. And everyone comes down hard, real hard, on Drissell. Say he ran a corrupt program, say he gave players grades and used them like pieces of meat, right?"

"Right."

"I'm reading the papers, reading all this shit about how bad the Maryland program was, how it should have never happened, and it hits me that if we'd gotten Bias, the same thing would have happened. And if he went somewhere else, the same thing. Wherever that young man went, the results would have been the same. You use people—you get what you can—and then you use new people. That's athletics. We would've given him grades and a car and whatever other shit he wanted and put the carpet out the whole way, and he would've dropped dead."

"There's no way to know that," I say.

"There is. Maryland wasn't the problem—the system's the problem. I can't feel clean in this game."

"So, I'm not clean?"

"This isn't personal. Why do people always take your decisions as a statement on theirs?" he says. "Why don't you drink?"

"Because I can't."

"Do you think alcohol is evil? Do you that no one should drink?"

"No," I say.

"I can't be in the business. Simple as that. I don't like who I am when I'm coaching." He raises his hands. "Got nothing to do with you, or anyone else."

"But you know the game."

"And that's why I want no part of it. The game is easy. Stay between your man and the hoop, see the ball, hit the open man, drop it in the basket. The game's beautiful. It's all the shit around it I don't want."

Terry goes to take care of the couple at the bar. He comes back. "You're making me feel kind of sleazy," I say. "I'm part of this now."

He shakes his head. "Don't mean it that way. You can help people. You can be good—it just takes an amount of work I'm not willing to put in." He takes a sip of coffee. "I gave the game all I had for thirty years. My body aches every morning. I can't sleep in one position for more than a couple of hours at a stretch. Thirty years, playing and coaching. Everything I had. Why do you think great players make shitty coaches and mediocre players make good ones? The great ones are done—they've done everything they can do."

"So I was mediocre? Thanks."

"No, but you were incomplete. You didn't get the career you should have. I did. Coaching was gravy. You're not done with the game." He shrugs. "I am."

"I wasn't mediocre," I say.

"Didn't say you were. That's not where I meant it to go," he says. "You were a hell of a player." He puts out his hand. "So, no. I'm honestly flattered, but I won't coach. Are we cool?"

I shake his hand. "We are. But I guess I should've asked my other question first."

"Which was?"

"I need a ref for tomorrow's scrimmage. Darnell's resting his legs and I only have ten bodies, so I have to play. I need someone with a whistle."

He thinks it over for a second. "You're not trying to sucker me?"

"I'm not," I say.

"OK. In a pinch, I'll help. Just no full time stuff."

"You're sure?" I say. "I don't want to force you into doing something you don't want to do."

"No one does, Bomber. Like I said, I got no trouble with the game, just the shit surrounding it. I can blow a whistle, play a little ref." He makes the offensive foul sign, the traveling sign. "No problem. You can play on that leg?"

"I rested it. The fluid's down. Just going to run up and down. Nothing fancy."

"Uh-huh. And when Money isolates on you on a wing, you going to do the smart thing and let him go? Or hurt yourself trying to prove you can still play with the kids?"

"Think I learned that lesson last time," I say.

≈40

I GO UP to my room and there's a message from The Chicken Man.
"Ben Thompson, do you play poker? My game needs a fourth for tomorrow. Call the office for directions to the house."

I flop on my bed and wonder what stakes Parcell plays for. He pays me—he knows I can't be losing money to him and his friends. Maybe he just wants to show off his toy. I turn on the TV and flip through the channels. Some sports cable station is showing some women's body-building competition. I stop and watch for a while. The women, all muscled and oiled under the light, remind me of Sean. Hard cut woman after hard cut woman poses out on the stage. I pick up the phone.

"Dream Dates," a woman says. "How may I help you?"

I feel stupid and awkward, like a kid calling for his first date. Like I'm going to get caught for doing something wrong. I hang up.

I mute the sound and watch for another minute before dialing again. The same woman answers.

"May I speak with Cassandra, please?" I say, wondering what she must think of me, and feeling like an idiot.

She pauses. "Cassandra's not here tonight. I could direct you to another lady who'd love to speak with you, or I could take your name and number for a call back." She says it all like the script it is—boredom tinged with annoyance. It's sad and arousing at the same time, her boredom.

I give her my name and number, even though Sean has the number.

"And a time?"

"Time?" I say.

"A time she can call you," she says.

"This time tomorrow should be fine," I say.

"Discretion?" she says.

"I don't follow," I say.

She takes a deep breath, acts like it's taking all the patience in the world to coach me through this. "Is there anyone there who, perhaps, shouldn't know Cassandra is calling you?"

On the TV, some woman accepts the heavyweight trophy. The screen reads: Next: Women's Pose Down.

"Discretion's not an issue," I say.

41

I DRIVE TERRY to practice. When we get there, Darnell's out on the floor with Money playing HORSE. Money's at the top of the key and calls a bank shot. He releases, takes a little arc off and it drops.

Terry whistles. "I love to watch him shoot."

"So does he," I say. "One of his problems—doesn't get back in transition quick enough. Too busy watching his shot."

Darnell bricks his. It gets glass and a little rim, but it's off line.

"Game, D," Money says. "You owe me twenty."

Terry and I walk up.

"Two-on-two?" Money says. "A buck a point?"

I turn to Darnell. "Thought you were sitting it out."

"Trying to play through it," he says.

"Don't push," I say.

"What about a game?" Money says.

"No," I say. "I can't afford you."

"I'll take you on my team, coach. I'll carry you. You'll make a few bucks."

"No go," I say.

Terry and I sit on the bleachers watching Money launch shot after shot until the team arrives and practice starts.

About five minutes into the scrimmage, I've got the ball on the left wing on a break. I don't know why, but instead of shooting a lay-up left-handed, I cut middle and go for the dunk. Everything feels great—all I can see is the rim—until I reach the peak of my jump much earlier than expected. I'm trapped in the air and I come at least four inches short. The ball hits the rim and I get snapped back on my ass. My head hits the wood hard. Play stops while I writhe around on the floor. The wind's knocked out of me and I see black. I hear voices, and I'm sure my eyes are open, but I can't see.

"Take five," Terry says. "Give him some air."

Slowly, shapes form and it's only dark in the corners of my vision like there's no floor or walls. Terry and Money help me up and over to the bleachers.

I nod, my sight returns to close to normal. I shake my head. "The basket's high."

Money laughs and slaps me on the shoulder. "One way to look at it, coach."

"You hurt?" Terry says.

"Just embarrassed," I say. Now that it's obvious I'm not hurt, everyone starts to laugh at me.

"What were you thinking?" Darnell says.

I feel stupid. "I don't know. Thinking it was ten years ago, I guess."

"It's not."

I tap my head. "Know that now. Just need these humiliating reminders."

The scrimmage starts again. Money's taking it easy on me. He'll beat me right, stop and pass off. He'll up-fake me, get a step, and pass off. After a while, he gets bored and takes a couple of shots. He hits two going right.

"Those decorative left arms cost less than the functional ones?" Terry says to Money. Money glares at him, and then at me.

The next time down the court, Money fakes me right and I take the bait. He blows by left on a pretty crossover and dunks over Darnell left-handed.

"Ain't no decorative fucking arm," he says as he runs up court. He points at his left arm.

"Great," I say to Terry. "He was going easy on me. Now you got him mad."

Terry shrugs. "He plays pretty when he's mad. I wanted to see it."

I turn and see Darnell limping off the court.

"You OK?" I say when I get over to him.

He winces with every step on his left leg.

"Knee?" I say. "Achilles?"

He drops to the floor. "Knee. Feels like razor blades in there."

I turn to the team. "That's it," I say. "Hit the showers. I'll see you at the shoot-around tomorrow."

I bend down. "Can you walk?"

He looks at me, then hangs his head. "Wouldn't be on the fucking floor if I could," he says quietly.

42

I CALL PARCELL and get directions and ask if I can bring Terry. He says he'd like that, he never got to thank Terry for the scouting trip. I ask Terry and, once I convince him that it's not another attempt to get him to coach, he agrees. We get to the house—a modern white three story overlooking the water—at seven-thirty. Parcell meets us at the door. He wears jeans and a white silk shirt that's untucked. It's the first time I've seen him in something other than a business suit or his TV Hee-Haw outfit. He looks strange.

"Ben Thompson, I'm glad you could make it." He shakes my hand and smiles. He looks at Terry. "Mr. Willis, good to see you."

Terry shakes his hand. "Same here, Mr. Parcell."

"Rube," he says and takes Terry by the shoulder. The house is spare and light—it's like one of those *House Beautiful* pictorials. It's as manicured as a golf course. The wall colors are all bright off whites and coral pastels; the furniture is chrome and black and modern. It's more casual, less imposing, than I'd imagined. He leads us through the living room and past a big-screen TV. Next to the TV are a stack of video tapes, all with Sarasota Sun and a date written on the spine.

"You have the games?" I say.

"Watch them all the time," he says. "Only a fool doesn't keep track of his investments. My secretary tapes them."

He leads us to a room off the main one.

"Ben Thompson, Terry Willis," he says. "John Parker and Leonard Craig." We shake hands. Parcell goes to the bar, pours himself a drink and gets me a mineral water.

"Mr. Willis?"

"Beer and Jack Daniels, if you've got it," Terry says.

Parcell smiles. "A man who drinks." He looks at me. "No offense, Ben Thompson."

"None taken," I say.

We sit and I look around. It's a game room with a nine foot Brunswick pool table, speed and heavy bag, a Soloflex machine, and the large round poker table. It's darker than the other rooms. A room of wood and green felt. Above both the pool table and poker table are old lights that look like the ones from Hollywood's version of a pool hall. Looks like we've walked onto the set of "The Hustler." A picture window overlooks the water. A lighthouse blips out on the horizon.

"Small stakes game," Parcell says. "Buck, five, ten. Hundred limit for the first two hours."

"This is small stakes?" I say.

"It is," Parcell says. "Just enough to make it interesting. To make it gambling. If there's nothing to lose, there's nothing to win." He shuffles. "How's my team?"

"Been better," I say. "We've lost Latimore for a week or two."

He frowns. "The heel?"

I shake my head. "Knee. He's pretty beat up."

"How bad?"

I shrug. "Bad enough."

"Should we cut him?"

I look at Terry and then back to Parcell. "What?"

"Should we fill his roster slot, Ben Thompson?" He leans forward. "You're headed for a championship in this league. Do you need another body?"

"He's not a body," I say. "He's my second best player and this is his last shot. There's no way I cut Darnell."

Parcell looks up at Craig and Parker. "Loyalty," he says.

I think I've passed another of Parcell's tests. He looks back at me.

"Loyalty's stupid." I shrink back in my chair and he deals the cards. "What would you do, Mr. Willis?"

Terry picks up his cards. "None of my business."

"You must have a opinion," Parcell says.

"I might," Terry says. "But that's none of your business."

"No offense," Parcell says. He holds his hands out in this I-won't-hurt-anyone gesture. "I asked your opinion. We're just talking."

"No," Terry says. "You're talking about someone's career. That ain't just talking." He looks at me like I'm part of this, like I knew the conversation would make this turn.

"I'll stick with what I've got," I say. "No new players."

We play a few hands. Parcell passes out cigars—Belicoso's—and we all smoke around his sucking ashtray—it's like the one from his office, but it's black. It whirls beneath the conversation. Smoke leaves my mouth, hovers for a moment, and disappears toward the table like its jumped off a cliff. Around the tenth hand, I finally win a few bucks, but I'm still down.

Parcell sips his drink. "So, you're seeing the topless cleaner?"

"How did you know that?" I say.

He taps his head. "A man that doesn't keep track of his investments is a fool, Ben Thompson."

"She's not really a topless cleaner," I say. "She's a writer."

"I stand corrected," he says. "No one is what they are. All the supermodels—they think they're actresses. The actors? They're directors. The bag boy at your supermarket? He's a screenwriter. She's not a top-less cleaner, she just plays one on TV." He looks at Craig and Parker. "This woman young Ben Thompson is seeing, she has holes all over her body."

They look confused. "Piercings," I say. "They're body piercings. Jewelry."

They still look confused.

"Holes. Voluntary holes in her body," Parcell says. "She's a nut. Be careful, Ben. A woman that puts holes in herself—what's she going to do to you?" He takes a puff of his cigar.

"Not normal," Parker says.

"There's no such thing as normal. Nothing's normal," I say.

"There sure as hell is normal," Parcell says. "I'm normal. Rest of the world's fucked up."

"Normal people don't own half a state," I say.

He points at Parker and Craig. "Three fifths of this table owns half a state. Sixty percent. A majority. That makes it normal."

"Around this table," Terry says. "Don't make it normal everywhere. Normal changes."

Parcell waves. "Fair enough," he says. "But, she seems dangerous to me, Ben Thompson." He deals the cards. "Just looking out for you. What would you do if she wanted to poke holes in you?"

I look at my cards—a pair of threes—and bet ten dollars. "Probably do it."

"You're kidding?" Craig says.

"If she wanted it, why not?"

"Shit would hurt," Terry says. "You're talking crazy."

I shrug. "Broke my nose four times. Broke every finger on my shooting hand. Ripped up my knee—had it drained maybe thirty times," I say. "That all hurt. Did all that for basketball. I could put a hole or two in me for her. I like her."

"You like her," Parcell says. "Fine. Take her out to dinner. Buy her some damn flowers. You do too many things for other people. You should stand up for yourself."

"I didn't let you cut Darnell," I say.

He nods. "I would have."

I look back at my cards and fold. "I know."

●43

ON THE DRIVE home, it starts to rain.

"That knock you took on the head," Terry says. "You were foolish. Trying to dunk."

"True."

"You won't do that again? Head shots take their toll, Ben."

"Understood," I say. I slow down to 55. The car slides over puddles of water, loses contact with the road a little too much for comfort. "Why all the concern?"

He says, "Your boss is a dangerous man."

"I know," I say. "That much I know. That's one of the reasons I wanted your help."

He whistles. "No way I could help you with that man." He's quiet for a moment and I hear the rain on the windshield and the hiss of the tires. "You want help? Cut yourself free from him as soon as you can."

"You think he's that bad?" I say. "He's just rich."

"He's bad news. Willing to cut Latimore's legs out from under him."

"You wanted me to trade Darnell," I say.

"Trade him, Bomber. Let him play somewhere else. That's one thing—that's a basketball decision. Making the team better. You trade him, he's still playing—you cut him and everybody wonders why. Thinks he's back on drugs. Cutting a guy because he got hurt? That's cold."

"It is," I say.

"Fucking medieval," he says. "He'll do the same to you, you know."

I hadn't really thought about it, but it's true. "Probably," I say. "He seems to like me, though, for some reason."

"Probably, shit. Be very careful. Don't trust him." He lights a cigarette and cracks the window. "He likes you? Everybody loved Darnell Latimore once. Everybody in the world."

44

I DROP TERRY off and get to The Palms at three in the morning. There are three messages beeping on the machine. I hit the button and drop down on my bed. The first is from Chucky Hoops—saying he'll be at tomorrow's game to scout Money again. He wants to see me after the game. The machine beeps and the second message comes on.

"This is Cassandra," Sean says. "I have a call-back for a Ben."

I'd forgotten about the poker game when I asked her to call back.

"Are you there?" she says. "Not screening me out, are you? It's not polite to tell people you'll be there, when you won't." She pauses a few seconds. "You can try me at 11 P.M. tomorrow," she says. "Last chance."

The next message clicks on and it's from Parcell.

"Ben Thompson, I'm sitting here watching the Baton Rouge game and a thought occurred to me. You don't wear good clothing. If I gave you a raise, would you dress like an adult? Go to a tailor and have yourself measured, for Christsakes. Wear a tie. Call me tomorrow."

45

THE RAIN HASN'T let up and there's flooding all over the West Coast. The team bus gets stuck behind accidents twice on the way to the gym. To my surprise, the Galveston Rangers made it. About ten minutes before the game, I pull Money aside.

"You've got eyes on you tonight," I say.

"I appreciate your telling me," he says. "What team?"

"No team. Chucky Chandler," I say. "Freelance."

"He carry any weight?"

"Enough," I say. "I know him—and you've got a good word from me." He looks surprised. "Don't get too excited. Just play your game."

He smiles. "What's the scoring record in this little league of ours?"

I look down and massage my temples. "Don't shoot for any records. Stay in control. Play within yourself."

He hold his hands out. "We're without D tonight, coach. You might need a scoring record out of me."

"Let's play it by ear, OK?"

He heads out on the court and I walk over to the bench. Darnell sits, his leg in a soft cast, extended to the baseline.

"You don't fit on the bench," I say.

"It's a new place for me," he says. "I haven't watched a game in years."

"You've never been hurt?"

He shakes his head. "Never."

I look out at the court. "You didn't watch when you were out of the game?"

"You mean when I was banned?" he says. "You can say it." He rubs the injured leg. "Nope. Never watched."

I sit next to him. "We'll miss you tonight."

"Nice to know."

Ten minutes into the game, we miss Darnell more than I'd thought. Part of the problem is Money. He's taking every shot they offer him—hasn't looked to drive or dish once—just bombing away from behind the three line. He stands there watching the shots, and they kill us in transition. At a time-out, I look up and see Chucky Hoops in the stands. He looks back at me and shakes his head. I yell at the team for a moment, then pull Money aside.

"You're the best in this league," I say. "Don't force it. Play your normal game. It's good enough."

He nods, but I can't tell if he's hearing me or not.

"Drive," I say. "Attack the rim. Get to the line. Don't settle for the J."

He looks over my shoulder and past me.

"Don't pull me out," he says. "I'll get in a groove."

"I won't pull you."

He heads back to the court and the game starts again.

"He's forcing," I say to Darnell.

"You blame him?"

"No."

Money starts to play a little better. His jumper's still off, but he starts to take it to the hole. About five minutes before half-time, Keller comes up with a steal and hits Hedda on the wing. She takes it up and

Pete Jones, their point guard, cuts her legs out from under her. She hits the floor flat on her back and doesn't move. I run out on the floor. She moves her legs and rolls over.

"You OK?"

She winces. "Lost my wind," she says. "I'll be all right."

Before I know what I'm doing, I run up to Jones.

"What the fuck was that?" I'm going after him and Keller is holding me back.

"A foul," Jones says and walks away.

"Fuck you, a foul. You cut her." I break free of Lewie's grasp. I push Jones in the chest. The ref steps between us. The benches empty and there's a mass of bodies under our hoop, pushing back and forth like two rugby teams. The ref gives me a technical.

"You're T-ing me?" I say. "What about Jones?"

"It's a flagrant. I made the call," he says and pushes me back. Lewie's got one arm and Money's got the other.

"That's bullshit," I say. "He could have paralyzed her and he gets a flagrant? That's fucking nuts. He should be kicked out. Have the guts to make the call. You're chickenshit."

"You're gone," the ref says and hits me with a second technical.

I start to calm down a little and pull free from Money and Keller. "I'm OK," I say. I turn to the ref. "It was a shitty call and you know it was a shitty call."

He waves at me the way grandparents wave good-bye to kids—with one hand opening and closing and this stupid grin on his face. Hedda's at the line, waiting to take her free throws. "You're OK?" I say.

"I'm fine," she says.

Before I head into the locker room, I walk over to Darnell. "They're all yours."

"I can't coach," he says.

"Just let them play," I say. "You'll be fine."

I head to the locker room and the fans—our fans—pelt me with cups of beer and chunks of hot dogs and garbage. I smell like a frat party by the time I get inside, my temper flares again, and I'm ready to punch somebody. I've never understood this mentality—some idiot pays five, ten, fifty bucks and figures it's his right to be a complete ass-hole for the evening. They ride me about my drinking, they ride

Darnell about his drugs, they ride Hedda for being a woman. You name it, they scream it.

A ticket and a seat gives them the right to shit on everyone on the court and none of them—none—knows what it takes to play the game.

The locker room is quiet. I sit on the bench. The floor is a thick epoxy gray—I must have painted a hundred floors like it. It's a sloppy job, the cut-in work around the baseboards is uneven. They didn't do the walls behind the heater. I hear the crowd cheer every once in a while and wonder how we're doing. A minute before half-time, a security guard comes in.

"You have to leave the locker room," he says.

"I'm kicked out of the whole gym?"

He shakes his head. "Just for half-time. I'll come get you after the team hits the floor."

I go out to the parking lot feeling like a kid who's been sent to the coat room to think about his behavior. Bad boy. Go to the corner, Ben Thompson. Stay away until you learn to play with the others.

The guard comes out the fire door.

"You can come in," he says.

"What's the score?" I say. We go inside.

"No idea," he says.

I sit on the bench and look up at him. He lights a cigarette and leans against the lockers.

"Could you check?" I say. "It's important to me."

He shifts his weight, leans against the lockers with the other shoulder. He holds his cigarette toward me. "Can it wait a minute?"

"Sure."

Late in the fourth, we're down five. The guard, whose name, I find out, is Randy, goes back and forth and gives me updates.

"You're down three," he says. "The girl's on the line." He goes away. We had a small crowd because of the rain and I can hear the ball bouncing, the squeak of the sneakers. "Tied up," he says. "Cash hit a three."

It eats me up—not being out there, but it's an interesting way to get the game. Randy comes inside. "Thirty seconds left. Looks like you might win."

Before I can ask him what, specifically, he means, he's gone out to the court again. A minute or two later, the team comes into the locker room. Keller and Hedda are first.

"Darnell's a natural, coach," Hedda says. "I'd be worried if I were you."

Money comes in and he's pissed. He kicks a locker, punches a wall, and heads to the men's. I follow him. He's slamming the stall door over and over. "Fuck. Fuck. Fuck," he screams with every slam. He looks at me. "Not now. Leave me alone."

Back in the locker room, Darnell walks up and gives me my clipboard. "All yours."

"Nice work," I say. "Thanks."

He raises his eyebrows and closes his eyes. "Didn't do a thing. Galveston sucks. They turned it over ten times in the fourth."

"What's with Kenny?" I say.

"He played like shit."

"How bad?"

"I would've pulled him if he wasn't being scouted," Darnell says. He looks down. "Maybe I should have."

I pat him on the shoulder. "Don't sweat it," I say. "You got me a win. I owe you."

46

CHUCKY CHANDLER is staying at the Holiday Inn and we meet at the bar. I check the stat line before I get out of my car. Money got 22, but he did it on 7-26 from the floor. One assist, only three rebounds. His worst game at the worst possible time. I head into the bar, ready to beg Chucky to look at him again. We shake hands.

"He had one bad game," I say.

Chucky holds up his hand. "I've seen him four times. I know that's not his game." He lights a cigarette. Chucky smokes in a hurry—the way guys who've been in prison or the army do it. Guys that had five minute breaks. They suck hard and deep, they never let the cigarette sit in the ashtray.

"So, he's OK?"

"He's fine. I can get him looks at three or four camps this fall. Could guarantee a European contract."

I shake my head. "He's been to Europe. He needs his shot."

"He can get it," Chucky says. "And he's got a shot, because he's got a shot. Tonight doesn't hurt that much. Not a good sign—the way he reacted to pressure—but it shouldn't hurt too much." He points at me with his cigarette hand. "You, however, fucked up tonight."

"I lost my cool," I say. "It was a shit call."

"Twice," he says and holds up his pinkie and ring fingers. "Twice you've gone ballistic over nothing. It looks bad."

"To who?"

"You don't get it, do you? You're being scouted, too, Thompson."

I lean back. It never occurred to me. "Really?" I say.

"There's CBA jobs. College, mostly division two, but some division one. Probably too late for this year," he says. "But people are looking. And you got to show more poise."

I nod, look down at the round deep walnut table. "So, Money's in good shape. I have to behave better." I take a sip of my drink. "What about Darnell?"

He looks surprised. "What about him?"

"What do you mean what about him? Is anyone interested."

He smiles one of those you're-so-dumb-it's-funny-smiles. "Thompson, one of the things working against you is that you picked him in the first place. Makes you look like a sucker. He's fool's gold. The book's closed on Latimore."

"This is your opinion?"

"It's everyone's opinion," he says. "Which makes it fact."

"He's still got game," I say.

"So what? I see a hundred guys a summer who've got game." He puts out his cigarette and lights another one. "Look, you want to hear this?"

"Probably not," I say.

"He's done. From the start he was a floater—head wasn't always in the game. He's a three-time loser who filled his body full of junk. He's finally, finally gotten straight—which people waited ten years for—and now his body's rebelling. You can't feed a body the crap he fed it and expect to stay healthy. Look at him now—breaking down midway through a twenty-eight game season. Shit." He shakes his head. "He's spent. I wouldn't risk my rep to get him a look, and neither would anyone else."

"You don't know him," I say. "He's a good kid."

"Great. He's a good kid. I deal in players, and he's a bad risk. Ten, hell, five years ago he was worth the risk. He's not anymore. There's no up-side to his game." He leans back. "So, he's a good person. He's clean. I'm happy for him. Wish him all the luck in the world, but that's as far as it goes."

A group of men and women dressed like bad parodies of cowboys and cowgirls come into the bar. The men all have these big cowboy hats that make their heads look like baseballs with ears. The women wear ruffled skirts that jettison from their hips at a stiff 45 degree angle. They look like those silhouettes they use on women's restroom doors with their hard triangular skirts.

"Fucking yahoos," Chucky says.

"What are they?"

"Line-dancing conventions. Whitest people on Earth—them and Mormons. They're fucking everywhere. I go to a new town, and it's full of cowboys." He takes a drag of his cigarette. "Every single fucking town. I can't shake them." He frowns. "I hate cowboys."

"I don't get them," I say. "Cowboys."

"What's to get?" Chucky says and points at the group putting together a bunch of tables. "They're morons."

47

I KNOCK on Money's door.

"Go the fuck away."

I knock again. "It's good news, Kenny."

He opens the door. "You going to kill that cow?"

"Better news."

I tell him what Chucky told me.

"What teams?"

"Not sure," I say. "Chucky seemed to think you could pick and choose a little."

He stands, resting against the open door. "Thought I blew it tonight."

"You didn't. But be more careful."

He nods. "You want to come in?"

I look at my watch and it's almost eleven. "Can't," I say. "Have some calls to make. Just wanted to let you know everything was cool."

He looks down for a moment, and looks back at me. "Thanks," he says. "I've been going nuts."

I hold my hand out and he takes it. "One bad game," I say. "Couldn't hurt you that much. You've made some noise here."

"I guess," he says.

"See you at practice," I say.

48

"SO WHAT turns you on?" she says.

"Listen," I say. "I'm still a little uncomfortable with this." I sit on the bed. "You go first."

"A lot of things turn me on," Sean says.

"Pick one." I lie flat on by back and stare at the ceiling. The line hums for a moment.

"When I was in school, I used to see this guy, Tom—a bartender—every Thursday night," she says. "It was nothing serious. Every Thursday, at midnight, I'd go and meet him and we'd go back to his place and fuck. We did this for a couple of months and, it was nice, but, it was nothing special and I was going to break it off."

"But you didn't?" I say.

"There was this other guy I knew from school. Nice guy. We'd have coffee every Friday before a film class and he kept asking about me and Tom—how we did it, where we did it and so on. He seemed really interested. So a couple months go by, and I'm about to break it off with Tom. And Stone says he wishes that I wouldn't."

"Stone?" I say.

"That was his name, OK? I didn't name him. Anyway, he tells me he has a confession. Tells me how much he looks forward to our little Friday discussions about me and Tom. How he goes home and jerks off thinking about us. And then—and he looks real shy—he asks me if he can come over to my house on Thursday nights. He wants me to tie him up—chain him to a bed or some furniture, go fuck with Tom for a few hours, and come home and tell him all about. No sex. No touching."

"And?"

"And I did it. Stone would come over at eleven-thirty. I'd tell him to strip, and lie on the bed. I'd chain his legs and handcuff his hands.

I'd get dressed in front of him and head over to meet Tom. And I'd fuck Tom, knowing the whole time, I had a guy chained up and home thinking about what we were doing."

"You didn't break up with Tom?" I say.

"Not then. It was fun. Every time I'd come home, there'd be Stone, all stretched out on my bed, chained up, with dried come all over his stomach. That turned me on, Ben. So, I'd undress in front of him, tell him what I did with Tom, and—more often than not—he'd come again. I'd untie him and he'd go home."

"You never slept with him?" I say.

"That wasn't our relationship," she says. "Then, Stone moved, and I broke it off with Tom."

"This is true?" I say.

"Of course."

"Who's telling me this?" I say. "Cassandra?"

"Sean," she says. "The story's true. Your turn, Ben. What turns you on?"

"That story did," I say.

"What about it?"

I don't say anything.

"You ever been tied up?" she says.

"A couple times," I say, and think of the last time—I was on a residential job and slept with the woman that lived next door to the job we were doing. She said she couldn't come unless I was tied to the bed, so I let her. "Not like that, though."

"And you liked it?"

"I did."

"You ever been spanked?"

"Spanked?" I say. "No."

"It feels great," she says. "Would you like to spank me, Ben?"

"You'd like that?"

"I would," she says.

"If you'd like it, sure."

"Why?"

"Because it turns you on," I say.

"Good answer," she says. "But we're still talking about me. So, you like being tied up. Do you like taking orders?"

I think for a moment. I'm worried that any of this will sound stupid and mundane next to Sean. "When I was sixteen, my sister—she's
two years older than me—went to this language school in Vermont.
Eight weeks, and they weren't allowed to speak anything but Russian,
or French, or whatever they were studying."

"What was your sister studying?"

"Russian. Anyway, she finishes her eight weeks, and brings back
two friends she met there. One, I forget, the other was this woman
named Sasha. She was attractive, and older."

"Older?"

"Eighteen, nineteen. Older at the time. They stayed at our house
for a couple days, and I was nuts about her—made a pest of myself,
following them around. Showing off. Being a jerk, pretty much. I figure there's not a chance—big difference between sixteen and nineteen,
you know?"

"True." she says.

"This isn't as dramatic as your tied-to-the-bed-come-on-the-
stomach story," I say. "But it applies in the taking orders sense. It's not
very dirty or dramatic."

"I'm interested. Go on."

"The last night Sasha and this other woman are at the house,
we're all in the basement watching a movie—Scarface."

"The original?"

I shake my head, even though I'm on the phone. "De Palma. Pacino.
So my sister and her friend fall asleep and it's just me and Sasha. Somehow, I never saw it coming, we start to make out. And it's nice—you
know? Quiet and kind of secretive. After a couple of minutes, she pulls
away. I had one of those sixteen year-old boy mustaches, you know?"

"Fuzzy. Thin," Sean says.

"Right. So she pulls away, and very nicely, but very firm, she says, 'I
don't like that. Go shave and come back.' I go upstairs and start to shave
and I notice that I'm excited, more excited than when we were just kissing. It was very direct: Do this and it will please me. I shave. I'm excited,
and bump some things on the counter and when I get back downstairs,
my sister's up. She stays up and watches the movie. I'm still hard and
frustrated and Sasha keeps looking over at me. She's in my dad's big
chair—the dad chair—and she's got an afghan over her lap and, after a
while I realize she's masturbating under the afghan. She stares at me the

whole time. Her hand moves faster and faster. Finally, she closes her eyes and shudders and comes. First time I'd seen anyone have an orgasm. The chair creaks a little, but my sister doesn't seem to notice."

"I like her," Sean says.

"So did I. After she's finished, she's blows me a kiss. The other friend wakes up, and I'm ready to kill her and my sister. Sasha goes upstairs to the kitchen. I think about following her, but figure it's too obvious. She comes back down and leans down to my ear. 'You look great,' she says. 'Thank you.' And that was it. She took off the next day."

The line is quiet for a moment. "You like taking orders, then?"

"I guess I do. In a sex sense, not a life sense."

"Shave between your legs before our next date."

"Really?"

"I said it nicely, but firm," she says. "I thought you liked that."

"I do."

"Good. Then you'll do it."

"If it's what you want," I say.

"Isn't this fun?" she says.

"Yes and no," I say. "But mostly yes."

"I'll see you tomorrow?" she says. "At the gallery?"

"You'll see me tomorrow."

49

AFTER PRACTICE, I find out Darnell's knee, which they thought was tendonitis, has a weak anterior cruciate. He's going in for more tests tomorrow, but he's definitely gone for two weeks and maybe longer. I drive to The Bunker and tell Terry.

"Bad news," he says.

"Worse," I say. "Chucky tells me there's no interest in him anywhere."

"None?"

"Apparently."

Terry shakes his head. "I'm sorry. I was hoping he'd prove me wrong and make it."

"Season's not over," I say. "He might still impress somebody and get a call."

"Not wearing a suit on the sidelines, he won't."

"True enough." I eat pretzels and watch the TV. Terry wipes down the bar.

"How's it going with your new lady friend?" he says.

"Good," I say. "Very good, I think. She's interesting. Never met anyone quite like her."

"How so?"

"She doesn't seem to get embarrassed. There's no shame in her."

"Opposites attract, huh?"

"She had me call her on her phone sex job."

"She does phone sex? And you called her?" he says.

"She does and I did." I take a sip of coffee.

"And?"

I shrug. "And we talked about sex."

"What about it?"

"What she likes, what I like. Traded stories."

He gives me this I-like-you-but-you're-nuts look and smiles. "As long as you're happy."

"I might be," I say.

 50

THE ART GALLERY is downtown on fourth street. I go with Sean and Hedda, wishing Sean and I were alone and staying in for the night. Sean drives—no one wanted to take my car. We park and head up to the entrance. Sean's wearing a short black mini-dress—I think it's silk—with spaghetti straps, and a pair of cowboy boots. Some well dressed people smoke out front—it seems to be a suit and dress crowd. I'm wearing one of my two coaching sports jackets and feel a bit out of place until I see Bone. He's got on a torn T-shirt with paint splattered all over it and a pair of faded Levi's with sandals.

"Thanks for coming," he says to us.

"How's it going?" Hedda says.

Bone shakes his head. "They've got me with a painter and a performance artist," he says. "Which is good, in a way—there's nothing to compare my work to."

"So what's the problem?" I say.

"The performance artist," he says. "You'll see when you get inside."

Sean says she wants to have a cigarette first. Bone takes Hedda in to show her around and I hang back with Sean. I can see the outline of her nipple rings through the silk, and I watch the fabric slide over them as she raises her hand to bring the cigarette to her lips. I start to get a hard-on, which feels strange after I've shaved—the skin is much more sensitive, and I can feel my cock and balls more than normal. She raises her arm, and shows me her armpit, which has a short growth of hair.

"I quit the cleaning," she says. "Letting it grow back."

"Looks nice," I say. Which it does—with the dress, it has a kind of a I-don't-care-what-you-think sexy arrogance. I look down and try to stop imagining us fucking.

"What's wrong?" she says.

"Can we go home?" I say.

She takes a drag of her cigarette, leans close to me and grabs my ass. "You want to go?"

"I do."

"Later," she says. "We promised we'd come look. You can wait, can't you?"

"I can," I say. "I just don't want to."

"Thanks for the compliment," she says.

I look toward the gallery. "I don't like friend's art," I say. "Friend's writing. Friend's children. Don't like anything I have to offer an opinion on."

"Friend's children?" she says.

"Anything they love that I have to judge. It's awkward. It's that anticipation, you know? If it sucks, what do I say? I don't want to be a jerk."

She lights another cigarette. "You really have a problem with what other people think of you, don't you?"

I lean against a big potted plant. It's an attempt to look casual, but the plant is top-heavy and it wobbles when I lean on it and I lose my balance for a moment. I think of all the people I've known who I disappointed, who hate me. They all liked me once, and I'm worried I'll fuck me and Sean up before it starts. I decide to try to be honest with her. "I do. Even people I hate, I want them to like me. I could have no respect for them or their opinion, but if I find out they don't like me, it bothers me."

Sean says, "Really?"

"Really."

"That's kind of sick."

"I know," I say.

We're about to go in, and Lewie Keller comes up with a woman. "Lewie," I say.

He shakes our hands. I introduce Sean.

"This is my wife, Kendra," he says.

I shake her hand. I try to think of something to say other than hello. "How do you like Sarasota?"

She seems quiet and shy. Lewie's one of the world-travelers in minor league ball. He's played in Turkey and Israel. Two or three stops in the states in two or three leagues. Pretty common resume, but it must be hell on families. "It's fine," she says.

"We need a new apartment," Lewie says. "Got to get away from those Mennonites."

Sean says, "Are they bothering you?"

"Strange people," he says. "We move here, I'm looking at maps for the best way to get around—I'm a map guy," he says and looks and Kendra.

"A map nut," she says.

"A map nut. And it looks like Twelfth Street is the center of it all, so I take a big apartment there without looking and the real estate people don't bother to tell me we're dead center in Mennonites."

"I hate Mennonites," Sean says. "Repressed lunatics."

"They are odd. Don't know if I hate them, but they make life difficult."

"They ride horses down our street," Kendra says.

"Horses?" I say. "Are they Amish?"

"They're Mennonites," Sean says. "It's the same, but different."

"What's the difference?"

"You'd have to ask them," Lewie says. "They seem pretty Amish. They don't like power tools—that's a pretty Amish thing to do. Dress like every day's a funeral. They hand out the leaflets, trying to get my kids to study at their school. Spooky folks." He shakes his head. "I want to move, but we're only here four or five more weeks."

"You know there's an Amish home page on the internet?" Sean says.

"Really?" Lewie says. "I don't get it."

"The Amish don't do it," she says. "Some guy maintains it—it's full of Amish facts and history. Kind of interesting."

No one talks for a moment. Every time that happens, I remember this one woman I knew in college who, whenever there was a lull in the conversation, would say, "Seven minute lull." People, at first, would ask her what she meant. She'd say that studies showed people couldn't talk for more than seven minutes without a silence. Whenever it happened—I knew her for a couple of years—she'd say, "Seven minute lull" when people were quiet. I can't remember another thing about her, not even her name.

It hits me for a second that I've known an awful lot of people in my life and I have no connection to most of them. No earth-shattering revelation—just a quick sad thought that goes away, but leaves an impression. Like when you're driving down the highway and—for no reason—you know, not just feel, but know you'll be dead someday. It's not news, but it leaves you kind of flat and dulled for a while.

Sean puts out her cigarette. "Should we go in?"

"Yeah," Lewie says. "Let's see what that crazy maintenance man is up to in his shed all night that keeps Money awake."

"This is a big night for Bone," Sean says. "The Peterson Gallery's a big deal." She looks at me. "Be nice. And be patient."

"I have no problem being nice," I say.

51

THE PERFORMANCE ARTIST is, I'm told, a woman. You can't tell, though. She's dressed as this strange mouse/rat creature. A big fuzzy suit with a rope for a tail. Furry slippers. She wears a fencing mask that has a tube out the side. The tube, Bone tells me, is so she can drink. The creature's name is Furry Friend. The gallery has the main room—with Bone's work and the paintings—and a back room where Furry Friend lives. She's done this room in a kind of frightening Appalachian cabin look. The inbreeders of "Deliverance" would feel at home.

"She lives in the gallery," Bone says. "Whenever she does a character, she stays in character the two weeks before the show, and the week after it."

"She's been in that rat suit for two weeks?" I say.

He nods.

Furry Friend is annoying. She doesn't talk, but she seems to enjoy wandering around making these honking noises. Sounds like a seal. Honk,

honk, honk. People in three-piece suits put their wine glasses down to hug Furry Friend. We wander around the gallery and people say:

"Have you seen Furry Friend?"

"Isn't Furry Friend great?"

Bone and I seem to be alone in our dislike of Furry Friend.

"That kind of crap cheapens what I do," he says. "That's what people think art is."

"It's stupid," I say. "But how does it cheapen what you do?"

"It cheapens everything," he says. He makes a stupid face talks like a moron, "I'm dressed up like a rat, isn't that brilliant? Where's my NEA?" He shakes his head. "Don't get me started. I'm going to grab a smoke. Want to come?"

"No," I say. "I'm going to look around."

He walks outside. I go to the bar and get a glass of water. It comes in a plastic cup with one ice cube. They give me one of those mini-napkins and I don't know what to do with it, so I put it in my pocket.

Bone's work, to my relief, is interesting. It's all made out of stuff he finds at junkyards, scrap houses, and in the garbage. Sean's in the corner by a piece called "Science."

The piece is built around two of those old chairs you used to see in beauty parlors—the kind with the big turquoise bubble that goes over your head. The two head bubbles are connected with wire and neon lights so that it looks like one of those brain-trading machines from an old science fiction movie. In one of the chairs is a mannequin. In the other is a mounted moose head. I think it's moose, anyway. It looks bigger than I imagine a deer to be, and the head is jammed up into the head compartment of the chair.

The chairs have newspaper and magazine articles glued to them. Like decoupage. I look closely—there's an article about the walking catfish—a scientific mutation. Another one is about a "Rambo-Fish" that marine biologists brought from Australia to lower the amount of Starfish on the coral reefs. The fish didn't have any natural enemies, it killed all the starfish, and then they found out starfish keep the coral reefs alive. The article is ripped, and that's all there is to it. There are headlines from tabloids and reputable papers. Mother Gives Birth to Giant Eye, says one. What Would Lincoln's Brain Tell Us? says another.

"I like it," Sean says.

"I love it," I say.

"Relieved?"

"Very much."

She hugs me and rubs up against me a little.

"How you doing?' she says.

"Better before you started that," I say.

She lets me go and we move on. There are a couple of other nice pieces. The lawnmower that Bone was working on the day he sprayed me with green paint is here. It's upside down on the floor. Welded to its blade is a pipe that has a blender mounted about three feet above the lawnmower. Both the blender and the lawnmower blade have what looks like red cottage cheese all over them. The title is on a card on the wall. It reads, "Warning: Keep Hands And Feet Away From the Mechanism During Operation." Mixed Medium. Artist: Bone.

I feel a hand on my shoulder. "Ben Thompson, how are you?" I turn and see Parcell.

"You came all the way down for this?"

He nods. "Joanna."

"It's Sean, really," she says.

"I know," he says. He looks at me. "So. What do you think of Bernard's work?"

"Bernard?" I say. "Is that Bone?"

"I refuse to call my nephew that silly name and I don't give a rat's ass whether he had it changed or not." He takes a puff of his cigar. A woman comes up and tells him there's no smoking. He looks at her for a moment, then turns back to us. "He's not bad, is he?"

"No. Pretty good," I say. "Course I don't know anything."

Parcell winces. "Stop that."

"Stop what?"

He points at me with his cigar. "Stop apologizing for your opinions. You're smart, Ben Thompson. You have every right to judge things."

The woman hasn't left. "Sir. Please put that out or go outside. It's the rules."

He turns and looks at her. "Fuck off," he says. She runs off like he'd threatened her. He winks at me. "They don't know any more than you. Stop apologizing."

"OK," I say. "Bone's work is good."

"Better," he says, and puts his hand around my shoulder. "I may buy some of his things."

"Me too," I say.

He laughs. "No, Ben Thompson. You can't afford it."

We're looking at some painting—simple stick figures around a dinner table. Nice, in an odd child-like way. Furry Friend comes up behind the three of us, honking.

"What the fuck is that?" Parcell says.

"Hi, Furry Friend," Sean says. It honks a couple of times and puts its hands out. "Do you want a hug?"

It nods and Sean hugs it. Furry Friend turns to me with its hands out. I look at Sean and, not knowing what else to do, I hug Furry Friend. It makes a couple of happy sounding honks and turns to Parcell with its hands out.

"Go away," he says. He turns to us. "What the fuck is this?"

Sean tells him. Furry Friend nods and honks while Sean fills him in on the art.

"You're stupid," Parcell says to Furry Friend. It makes a sad honk. "Go away."

Furry Friend holds its ground.

"I'm trying to appreciate people that work for a living," Parcell says. Furry Friend shakes its head as if to say Parcell doesn't get it. "You are a sad pathetic little person in a rat suit. Now go away."

Furry Friend drops its head and shuffles slowly away. People next to us that saw the whole exchange walk up to hug the artist. They look at Parcell like he's ruined the party. "You're fools," he says. He points at Furry Friend. "That is silly and a waste of space and you know it, but you're all too polite to say a thing. If I had my way, she'd lose a finger."

He looks back at me and smiles. "Never be afraid to offer an opinion, Ben Thompson. They may not like it, but people respect conviction."

52

"YOUR BOSS IS a sad man," Sean says. She cuffs my hands behind the bedpost. "Afraid of what he doesn't understand."

"You understood Furry Friend?" I say.

"I did not," she says. "I don't even know if it was supposed to be understood. But I wasn't afraid of it." She unbuckles my pants and pulls them down. She looks at my crotch. I can feel the breeze—it's cold where I used to have hair. "Very nice. Are you afraid of what you don't understand?"

She ties my left leg down. "Probably," I say.

She stands up. "Do you want to stop?"

"No."

She ties my right leg down. "Try to move," she says. I move a little, but not much. "Good," she says and takes off her dress over her head. She's naked except for her cowboy boots. She straddles my chest.

"Isn't this fun?" she says.

"Yes."

She smiles, gets off of me and walks to the table by the window. She takes a vibrator out of her purse and gets back on top of me.

"Did Bone do that?" I say.

"My clit piercing?" she says.

I nod.

"Say it," she says.

"Did Bone do your clit piercing?"

"That wasn't so hard, was it?" She leans down and kisses me. "You're fun."

"Did he?"

"No. He's very professional—it's not a comment on him. But I wanted a girl to do it. Someone who knew a little more about it." She runs the vibrator over the silver barbell and it clanks against the metal. "Do you like it?" she says.

"I do. Very pretty."

"It's great with the vibrator," she says and closes her eyes. "Just heavy enough to rattle against everything. Now be quiet and watch me."

"I am watching you," I say.

She puts a finger to my lips and masturbates on my chest. When she comes, her legs squeeze tightly against my ribs. She collapses on top of me and kisses me.

"I needed that," she says. "Thank you."

"No problem," I say. "I didn't do too much."

"You did plenty," she says. "Where are your keys?"

"In my pants. Why?"

Sean gets up and puts her dress back on. She grabs my keys.

"I'm going to get a drink," she says. "I'll be back."

She leaves and I think it's a joke until I hear her boots clumping down the stairs.

I'm there, on the bed, thinking she's gone down to her car or something. After a couple of minutes, it hits me that I don't know her that well, and she might not be coming back. We seem to have hit it off, but she could be nuts, or mean, and I could be here all night. I fight against the cuffs and they cut hard into my wrists. About ten minutes later, the phone rings.

"Ben Thompson is not in at the moment. Please state your business, time of call and phone number, and he'll get back to you as soon as he can. If you're calling about Sarasota Sun tickets, dial 1-800-SARASUN for the most exciting action on the coast."

It beeps.

"You're an odd man, Ben, to have someone else's voice on your machine," Sean says. When I hear her voice, I start to relax. This is still part of the game. "I'm down at Terry's bar and I thought I'd see if you wanted to meet us." She pauses. "But I guess you're in for the night." She must be calling from the bar phone, because I can make out voices that sound very close to her. I hear Bone's laugh. Sean says, "It's too bad you can't make it, Ben. Everyone's here." The voices get a little farther away and quieter, so my guess is she's moved a little away from them. "Pleasure, Ben Thompson," she says, "is eternally deferred. See you soon."

The phone machine whirls and clicks and the red light flashes every five seconds to let me know I've got a call.

My hands and feet start to go tingly numb. I'm tied pretty tight and I've got pains in muscles I didn't know I had. My arms shake for a while and I fight it. I try to get into a comfortable position, but it's no use. I give up start to relax and go with the pain, instead of against it, and it starts to feel good. It still hurts, but it's got a nice burn to it.

For a few minutes, I picture Sean coming back and stripping naked. I play out her masturbating on my chest a few times. After a while, though, my mind drifts and I feel a little guilty. It seems like a violation—a minor cheating—of this situation, in a way. Like I'm under some kind of obligation to think about sex. I hear footsteps on the stairs and think it's her, but it's not. It's one of the players going to their room.

Then it hits me that I could get caught like this. I've been robbed twice in my life—what if someone walks in? What if there's a fire? I watch the red light on my answering machine go on and off. Every once in a while, I have a muscle spasm in my arms or legs, and—after every one—it's like someone gently stroked my cock. A weird sensation.

I hear the doorknob turn. She comes in, puts a finger to her lips, and gets on top of me. "Don't say a word," she says.

She goes down on me. It's very slow and teasing. Every time I'm about to come, she stops. She moves up, sits high on my chest, her legs around my head.

"Lick me," she says. "Make me come."

And it's fun and strange—she's soft, wet, and warm, with these cold little metal balls clanking against my teeth, running hard as BB's on my tongue. When she comes, she grabs my head and pulls me closer to her. She grinds against my face and lips and I hear the cartilage in my nose scrunch under the pressure.

She kisses me, slides down my body until she's between my legs, and starts teasing me again.

This goes on for about an hour, and near the end, I've lost all control and it's kind of scary—I see parts of me shaking and thrashing, but I couldn't stop them if I wanted to. Finally, she lets me come. She unties me, and lies down next to me, smiling.

"You're not mad?" she says.

"No," I say. "Little sore." The feeling starts to come back in my hands and feet. They tingle whenever I move. "Not mad."

"I'll let you get back at me next time," she says. "You can tie me up and go away."

"Next time?" I say.

"You're fun."

"So are you," I say.

We stay together, kissing for a while, and I turn on the TV. We watch crap and make fun of it. The same infomercials as always are on.

"Can you find the hair-sucking one?" she says. "I love that."

I click around. "I can try."

She leans close, kisses me on the cheek. "Can I stay the night?"

"Of course."

I can't find the suck-hair machine one, so we settle for "American Gladiators."

"Almost as good," she says. "The boys are dull, though. They should just have the chick gladiators."

"I've got a road trip starting tomorrow," I say. "A week."

"And?" she says.

"And I'll miss you, is all. Can I call you?"

She kisses me. "You can and you should." She writes down a number. She smiles. "Call me at home, though, OK?"

"Home. I've moved up in the world," I say.

"You have," she says.

53

WITHOUT DARNELL, we're just not that good a team. There's no consistency to the games—if Money's hitting, we can hang around and have a shot at the end; if he's cold, we're dead. Losing is miserable—you have control and you don't. Still, we patch together two wins against four loses heading into Galveston—the last stop on the trip.

We took a bus out of Sarasota, and we're supposed to fly back out of Galveston tonight after the game. I feel like I swallowed bowling balls—it's impossible to eat right on the road. Greasy this and fried that, and everything's cooked in lard. Most of the players eat meat—me and Hedda are the only vegetarians—so they don't have too much trouble. Hedda and me, though, we go through the yellow pages in every ratshit town, calling restaurants.

"Are your beans fried in lard?" we say.

"Lard?" they say like it's a foreign word. "I don't know."

There is a pause—every town this happens. "Could you check?"

And they do, and it's always fried in lard. We eat eggs and salads in every town. I think it's bad for the psyche, that same meal day after day. I call Sean and The Chicken Man from every stop. Sean tells me Bone sold two pieces from the show. He's filling the pool with water and doing all kinds of work at The Palms. She says I'll be amazed. I try to steer the conversation around to us, try to get a gauge on how she feels about me, but I can't. She just gives me news—nothing personal and I know I'll spend the rest of the trip wondering if I did something wrong.

I call Parcell from a rest stop and he tells me he has big news and that I have to come see him when we hit town.

"What is it?" I say.

"Not news for the phone, Ben Thompson. I need to see you." Cars hiss by on route 10. "I can't hear you, Ben Thompson. Where are you?"

"Outside Lake Charles," I say. "On the road."

"Lake Charles? Beautiful town. Too bad you can't stay a while. I own birds there."

I smash the receiver to my ear, not sure if I'm hearing him right. "Birds? You mean chickens?"

"Birds, Ben Thompson. Chickens aren't birds, they're poultry. Birds, exotic birds. Colorful, talkative things. Importing business," he says. "You want a bird?"

"I don't think so," I say.

"I can get you a fine bird," he says. "To celebrate the news. You could work for me for five years and still not be able to afford one of these birds. Think about it."

"I'm not a bird guy," I say. "What's the big news?"

"When you get here, Ben Thompson. Come see me."

54

AT GALVESTON, the crowd's small again. We're shooting warm-ups on our end of the floor. Darnell sits next to me on the bench. He's out at least one more week.

Jammin' Ranger, the Galveston mascot tries to work the meager crowd into a frenzy about a half hour before the game. He's dressed in a sort of Village People meets The Lone Ranger costume—it's an old Texas Ranger outfit, but his pants are neon blue, and his mask is sort of a glittery red, the color of Dorothy's shoes in The Wizard of Oz. His hat is that blinding white that fluorescent lights make when you have a hangover—so bright you feel it sting and jackhammer at the back of your eyeballs. The P.A. announcer introduces him, and Jammin' Ranger runs out on the court with his guns firing blanks. Bang, bang, bang. He grabs a ball and runs, hits this mini-trampoline out by the foul line, and slams a monster dunk down.

"Sign him up," Darnell says. "Cowboy's got some moves."

"He's no good without his trampoline," I say. "Can't use him."

Jammin' Ranger moves the trampoline back to the top of the key. It's kind of pathetic—what little crowd there is couldn't care less. It's so quiet, I can hear bits of conversations behind us. He begins his run on our side of the court. Some of our team turn to watch. He runs up and hits the tramp at full speed. His jump looks wrong from the start—he's flying off right a bit; his legs are out from under him—and he hits the backboard with the side of his body and crumples to the floor like he's been shot. His hat goes flying in a white blur. When he hits the floor, it sounds like a big fish thwacked on a boat deck—a hard, wet, painful sound.

"Fuck," Darnell says.

He and I get up and run over to the ranger. His arm's broken, and splintered bone has ripped through the skin of his forearm. He rolls around for a second or two making these painful grunts. He looks at his arm and throws up—some of it hits my pants and shoes. His eyes dance and roll a little and he passes out.

"Doctor," Darnell yells. "We need a fucking doctor here."

The team comes down.

I bend down toward the ranger.

"Don't move him, coach," Hedda says.

Darnell must have gone into the locker room because Galveston's coach, Billy Coleman, comes out.

"What happened?" he says.

I tell him.

He shakes his head. "What a night."

We wait a few minutes. The paramedics come and take the ranger away. I go and pick up his hat and give it to one of them.

"What's this?" she says.

"His hat," I say.

She takes it from me, gives me this funny look that says my priorities are out of order, and leaves with the rest of them.

Billy Coleman puts his arm around my shoulder. "We have to talk."

"What's up?"

He takes me over to the side of the bleachers. "I was coming out to tell you before all this," he says and points to the spot where the mascot went down. "We're done, Ben. Team's gone."

"What?"

He looks tired. "We haven't been paid in two weeks—me or the team. I get a call from Tom Davis—majority owner—today. We've folded."

"Shit," I say.

"They closed up shop."

"I don't get it," I say. "They can do that?"

He holds his hands out, tilts his head to one side. "They can do anything they want." He shakes his head. "Idiots thought they'd make money." He laughs a quiet, tired laugh. "In The Gulf Coast League."

"I'm sorry, Billy." I look at him, hear the bounce of the ball on the floor. "Where's your team."

"Gone," he says. "They talked some shit about a class-action suit. But, they're back at our hotel. Probably calling their agents."

"What are you going to do?"

He shakes his head. "No fucking idea. Work for someone who pays me, I hope. Like to stay in the game. Maybe go back to scouting. Maybe try to coach in Europe." He looks at the floor and back at me. "No idea."

"This sucks," I say.

"Breaks of the game, right?" He slaps me on the shoulder and walks away.

I go out to the court and tell the team the news. As I'm telling them, it comes over the P.A. that the game is canceled and The Galveston Rangers are no more. They announce that refunds are available at the ticket office. In a minute or two, it's just us in the gym. Some of the players head toward the locker room.

"I came here to play," Money says. He holds up a ball. "Lewie? Anyone?"

"I'm tired," Lewie says. "I'm going back to the hotel. See you at the airport."

"No one wants to play?" Money says. "You people are sad." He looks at me. "How about a practice, coach? Let's scrimmage."

"Normal people get tired, Kenny. Let them go."

"I'll hang out," Hedda says.

The team changes and hits the bus. Darnell and I hang back; sit on the sidelines while Money and Hedda play one-on-one. Money hits four or five jumpers in a row. I've been around him long enough to take it for granted, but every once in a while, it hits me how gorgeous his shot is.

"Money's talking about getting some looks," Darnell says.

I nod. "Jersey. Atlanta. A few others."

Hedda has the ball and she puts Money behind her and backs him into the paint. She hits a pretty up-and-under scoop shot off glass.

"Pretty," he says. "Adrian Dantley. She plays big like him."

"I wish," I say. "She's no Dantley."

"Didn't say she was. She reminds me of him, the way she uses the body."

"You play against him?"

He shakes his head. "He broke his leg my rookie year. But I saw him before that. A midget for a forward, but he could score on anyone."

Money gets a rebound and takes it out to the three line and drains a jumper.

"Never seen a shooter like him," I say.

"There's a bunch of them," Darnell says.

"Not that good."

"Almost that good."

We watch them play for a couple of minutes.

"Thanks for not cutting me," Darnell says.

I look at him. "What did you hear?"

"Nothing. I've been around. A lot of people would have let me go, and I don't figure it was the folks with the cash that kept me around." He looks at me for a moment, and looks out at the court. "Money's getting looks. Hedda's got a European deal wrapped in the women's league. Lewie, probably CBA. If anyone were interested in me, I would have heard by now. I can't play—may need surgery—I make more money than most of the team, and no one else wants me. Don't take a rocket scientist to figure out that someone might have thought of cutting me."

The janitor comes in and says that he's got to cut the lights. He tells Money and Hedda this.

"Five minutes?" Money says.

"I got a chance to get home early," the janitor says. "Closing time."

Money and Hedda keep playing. The janitor goes over to the far wall and sticks that little key into the light switch and half the power is cut. The regular lights stay on, but the court lights are cut, and it's fall-out shelter dim. Money's shot falls.

"Don't need no lights," he says. "I know where the hoop is. Radar, baby."

I tell them to hit the showers. I ask the janitor if we can wait and he nods. Money and Hedda head to the locker rooms.

"We'll get a cab," I say. "Get something to eat."

The gym is dark. It's just me and Darnell in the bleachers on our side. On the other side, the janitor goes through the seats, putting bits of garbage into a Hefty bag.

"So why didn't you let me go?" Darnell says.

"Cutting you never came up," I say.

"Don't lie to me."

"It came up," I say. "But I thought it was stupid. You don't cut a player like you."

"I'm not the player I was," he says. "I feel it. Can't do what I did—even before the injury. I'm not me anymore."

I turn to him. "I've been sticking up for you the whole season. Defending you. What are you telling me?"

"Nothing," he says. "I appreciate it—your sticking up for me—but I didn't ask for it." He takes a deep breath. "I'm tired, coach. I've been clean for three years and played in five leagues trying to make it back, and I'm not sure why. You look at Money—he'd play in an empty gym for nothing. He loves the game. Hedda, Lewie, Childs—same thing." He leans forward. "I could never pick up another basketball and be happy."

"You're talking shit," I say. "You're just depressed—you've never been injured."

"No. Thought this before I got hurt. Took me all these years to realize I don't like basketball that much—don't know if I ever did."

"I don't buy it," I say. "There's no way—absolutely no way—you could have been the player you were without loving the game. You don't get that good at something you don't like."

"I liked being the best at something," he says. "Don't know if I ever loved what I was best at and I haven't been the best for a while." Hedda comes out of the locker room—she's across the court from us, 30 or 40 feet. "I think I would have been better off being good at something else."

I stand up. "What?"

"Nothing specific," he says. "Just something else."

I shake my head. He's just being honest, but I'm angry. You don't piss on talent the way he has. But, who am I to tell him what he should love?

Money comes out a couple of minutes later and we start to leave the gym. The janitor has put on those little rubber gloves they use in hospitals, and he's mopping up the blood and vomit from the court where the mascot fell. I look down and some of the vomit's dried and crusted on my shoe.

✦55

I GET HOME and there's a message from Chucky Chandler about Money getting tryouts. There's a call from Claude, my ex-brother-in-law, about our painting business. He's having trouble getting a check out of some contractor. On the table by the window is a rose in a paper cup. Underneath is a note—a little damp from the water seeping out of the cup.

Welcome home. Missed you. PS. Bone let me in. Hope you don't mind. Sean.

I look at it and feel better, but I wonder why she couldn't have told me this when I talked to her.

✦56

"BEN THOMPSON, how are you?" Parcell stands and comes over to me as I enter his office. There's a Mennonite woman—plump and middle aged—cleaning over by the bar. She's dressed in blacks and grays, has what looks like a coffee filter on her head.

"No more topless cleaners?" I say, and the woman turns and gives me a strange look.

"Every Tuesday, Ben Thompson." He sits and motions for me to do the same. "Every Thursday, she comes in and really cleans." He leans forward. "You're not paying for the cleaning with the other service."

"Makes sense." I look out the window. It's a cloudless day and the sky is robin's egg blue for what seems like forever. "So what's the news?"

"First things first, Ben Thompson. Galveston's folded."

"I know," I say. "I was there when it happened."

He frowns. "No. You were there to see the result of what happened—a part of it, anyway. It's been happening for quite some time. I tried to buy the team, but they wouldn't let me own two. I tried to tell them it's bad for the league—looks second rate to have teams dropping like that."

"Sign of a bush league," I say.

"Precisely," he says. "Bad for the league, bad for the image—bad for the young men on that team."

I remember the look on Billy Coleman's face when he told me he had no idea what he was going to do. "True enough."

"The ten Galveston players are in a dispersal pool. The owners came up with this—worst team picks first. We're in second, so we're picking sixth. Do you want to fill the roster slot?"

I shake my head. "Sixth man on Galveston isn't worth picking up." I cross my legs. "Clark, maybe Harden are worth something, but they'd go one, two. Nothing beyond that."

"Still sticking with your boy?"

"Latimore?" I say.

He nods.

"Yes and no. It's personal, but it's practical, too. Half of Darnell can get us to the finals. Not a player on the Galveston roster other than Clark—who we have no shot at—who could do that." I'm drawing on my sneaker with a pen, passing time—I feel like I'm back in school. "Makes no sense."

"Don't be loyal, Ben. It's dumber than revenge." He looks at me with concern. "I understand the impulse, but you're wrong."

I look up from my sneaker. "Do you know more about basketball than me?"

"I do not, Ben Thompson." He looks hard at me. "Do you know losers better than me?"

I rub my neck. My hand passes over a scar I got when I was too drunk to stand over a urinal. Slit my neck down to the bone on some external plumbing. Bones aren't white when they're in you—they're not like those biology skeletons. They're more of a creamy living color. I fell in a puddle of piss, didn't clean it or get it stitched, and my neck was infected for a few weeks. "I might," I say.

"You do not," he says.

"I was a loser," I say.

He waves my comment off like a traffic cop saying: Stop. "You were off-track. You were not a loser."

The cleaning woman finishes and leaves. I watch her go, turn and look out the window. "What's this about?" I say.

"About?"

"You and me. I don't get you. What's the deal? Why the high opinion? What's your investment in this?"

"You need to know?"

"I'd like to know. Why me in the first place? You could've had any number of coaches."

"Fair enough, Ben Thompson." He puffs on his cigar. "I saw you play in college whenever I could. Thought you'd be something in the pros. I loved your game."

"That's it?" I say.

"I followed you. Talked to scouts. Heard what you went through after the surgeries. People admired you."

"When?"

"Chicago. '84 pre-draft camps."

"I couldn't pay anyone for a tryout at that camp."

"That's not the point. You worked when it was stupid to keep working. And you failed, failed and failed," he says. "I was in a position to help you and, I might add, have some fun. Always wanted to own a team. When I bought one, I hired you."

"Because you liked the way I played fifteen years ago?"

"That was part of it," he says. "The rest is none of your business. If more than two people know you did a good thing, you did it for the wrong reason." He leans back and his chair creaks that rich leather creak. "Why are you sticking with Latimore?"

"Because he can help me."

"That's a lie and you know it, Ben Thompson. Why did you draft him?"

"Because he was one of the best I'd ever seen."

"Was. Listen to yourself. Was. That's the wrong tense."

"He's still got game," I say.

"Stop it. Stop lying to me. Stop lying to yourself. He does not have game. Hell, he can't even play and we've got a knee expert that says he's on his last leg, so stop this nonsense. Stop feeding strays and giving change to every nut-job wearing tin foil to protect them from aliens. People will suck you dry if you let them. You are a coach. Listen to me, Ben Thompson. I'm helping you."

"You're full of shit," I say. "I'm not lying to you—I've forgotten more about the game than you'll ever know. If I say he's got game, as far as you're concerned, he does. That was our deal. I handle the game—you handle the money."

"True," he says calmly. "But it's my money that pays for your game. It's not as simple as you make it. The money and the game—they're not mutually exclusive."

"I won't cut him. Fire me, do whatever you want, but he stays. This is my decision." I stand up. "Are we done?"

"I hope not," he says. "Sit." He looks up. "I won't cut him. Sit."

I sit down.

"Before our conversation took an ugly turn, I was going to tell you something. Craig and Parker. You played poker with them."

"Right," I say.

"Don't pout, Ben Thompson. You're wrong here, but I'll let you be wrong. Keep your loser. Craig and Parker own, or owned, the Syracuse Blizzard."

"The CBA Blizzard?"

He nods. "One and the same. It's mine."

"I'm unclear."

"I bought the Blizzard. Moving them lock, stock and barrel to Florida." He re-lights his cigar. "I need a coach." He puffs to get the cigar going—rolls it over the flame. "What do you say?"

The CBA—a step away from the NBA. Real players and full rosters. A full season—56 games. I think for a moment about what Chucky said about me being scouted. No matter what, though, I probably wouldn't do better than this. But more of these arguments, more push and shove with Parcell.

"Can I think about it?" I say.

"What's to think about?" he says.

I decide not to re-hash the who's in charge argument. We both know it's his show and that Latimore could be gone in one phone call from The Chicken Man. "Where are you going to play?" I say. "Can't have a CBA franchise in that gym."

"We're going to have to move it up here to Tampa, " he says. "But you can still stay down in Sarasota. Not much of a drive, Ben Thompson." He frowns. "You're talking details much too soon, here. There will be a place to play, there will be players, there will be an assistant coaching slot, a trainer—all the fringes. You'll have a raise. But let's not talk details now. Do you want it?"

My stomach drops. I think of painting condo developments until I'm sixty. Painting is one of those jobs that kills you slowly—it offers just enough variety for you to think you're not stuck. I flash on Lobster Boy and his whisky and TV trays and a sad dull life. My empty life back in Miami. "Yes," I say. "I think I do."

"Coach Ben Thompson." He shakes my hand. "You've made the right decision."

I turn and walk out of his office, hoping that he's right.

⚇57

HEDDA MAKES THE "News and Notes" section of *The Sporting News*. It's a small article, but it doesn't treat her like a total circus freak. I'm out by the pool reading it. Bone's filled it with water and it looks like a real pool, except for the old diving board.

"Everyone's been great," she says in the article. "I had trouble adjusting—more off the court than on. It took a while to convince them I could play. But, they treat me like a player now."

I put the paper down, wondering how strange it must be for her. Ann Meyers signed a contract with The Pacers in the 70's, but she didn't make the roster. Nancy Lieberman-Cline played in a minor league. There was that woman goalie in hockey. Not much precedent for what she's done. I see Sean coming from the parking lot.

"Hey stranger," she says.

"Hey."

"What's wrong?" she says. "Thought you'd be happy to see me."

"I wasn't sure you'd be happy to see me."

"You didn't get my note?"

"I got it," I say. "You just seemed kind of distant on the phone."

She takes a deep breath. "We're not married." She sits next to my chair. "I like you, Ben. But I'm not a be-there-all-the-time kind of person. I need to be alone a lot." She rubs my arm "OK?"

I sit there for a minute, thinking she's worth more than a couple of personality quirks. "OK." I hold up the paper. "My players are getting ink."

"Saw it," she says. "They don't mention you."

I shrug. "I'm nobody. The reporter asked me some questions about her, but I must not have said anything worthwhile."

"What did you say?"

"That she's a legitimate player, but she's got real problems with her body. They asked me if I thought she could go pro—big-time— and I said no. Don't think it fit the tone they wanted."

"You don't think a woman could make the NBA?"

"Someday," I say. "But she'll probably be a guard. A quick one. Not a power forward."

She frowns, but it's not her you're-a-sexist-asshole frown, more of a world-isn't-fair one. She bends down and kisses me lightly. "Missed you," she says. "Really."

"Same here," I say.

We go down to The Bunker. Terry waves—he's talking to some old man in overalls at the bar. He looks over.

"Coffee," I say.

"Tequila," Sean says.

Terry looks at his watch, raises his eyebrows. He gets the bottle. "Training wheels with that?"

"Straight," she says. She turns to me. "We're celebrating."

"We are?" I say.

"I sold a piece," she says. "Two, actually. One's a great resume piece. The other one pays."

"Really," Terry says. "Congratulations."

I pat her on the back, let my hand rest there for a moment, rub it in circles. "What'd you sell?"

"A French Feminist piece about alternating roles of power and gender in the workplace—the absence of a center in pseudo democracies," she says. "And another that's a sort of diary of a phone sex operator thing."

I sip my coffee. "I wonder which one paid."

"Don't think too hard," she says.

The guy at the bar drinks a beer and looks teary-eyed at the bottles behind the bar. Looks like he's been plucked out of a country song. He's thin and beaten-looking. The kind of guy they always seem to do TV interviews with after hurricanes. When the flood comes, he's up on his roof. He's staying put. That kind of guy. Sean shakes his hand and introduces herself.

"Dan Toller," he says. "Your neighbor." He points at me.

"The man with the eggs?" I say.

He nods, and points to his empty beer glass. Terry gives him a refill.

"You OK?" Sean says.

It's a question I wouldn't have thought about asking—none of my business and the answer's probably long and sorrowful—but she has this quality of being able to talk to anybody. Her IQ's got to run circles around most people, but she seems interested in them. Weird. If I were that smart, I don't think I'd be that interested in the world.

"Elaine," he says. "Had to put her down."

"Elaine?"

"She was sick—lame to begin with, wasn't supposed to make it—Brucellosis," he says.

"A cow?" Sean says.

"She was lame at birth," he says. "Blind and stupid—dumb for a cow, and cows are not smart animals." He drinks his beer. "But she was family. The kids loved her." He takes a breath and lets it out slowly. "Shot her this morning."

"Why'd you shoot her?" I say.

He looks at me. "She was sick. Suffering."

"No," I say. "Why didn't you put her to sleep? Have a vet do it?"

He laughs and looks at Sean. "Your friend ain't from here, is he?"

"City boy," Sean says.

"You don't put them to sleep," he says. "They ain't cats or gerbils. And a vet costs a hell of a lot of money." He's explaining this to me like I'm a dumb kid, but he's upset, and I let him lecture me. "Besides, she was family. Wouldn't be right to have some nobody do it. Family deserves to be put down by family."

"That makes sense," Sean says.

I look at her, thinking: it does? How does that make sense?

"I'd expect the same," Toller says. He points at his chest. "I got a bad heart. Wall trouble. Other organs too. Got spots on the inside that are as thin as wax paper to hear the doctors tell it."

I'm worried we're going to get a life story here, that I'll be stuck to this barstool three hours from now hearing how the country's gone to hell and the fat cats in Washington don't give a shit, and all the other crap you hear in bars from strangers. Shit that's true, but tired. Spent air. I look at Terry and Sean and they seem to be interested so I don't say anything.

Toller makes circles with his index finger that follow the condensation ring left from his glass. He's missing the thumb on his right hand. There's a pinkish yellow indentation where the thumb should be, all lumpy and hard looking. "Had me in for tests a while back. Tubes coming and going. They want me in for more, but it ain't happening. No way for a man to be." He takes another deep breath and looks at me. "No. I did the right thing. She was suffering. I'd want the same."

"It must have been difficult," Sean says.

He looks at her and seems touched—like he's met someone who understands him. "It was."

# 58

SEAN AND I run into Money out by the pool. He's in a reclining chair that Bone's painted shocking pink. The place is taking on a surreal look—there's gravel leading up from the driveway to the pool and he's painted that, too. I've seen him do it—he takes a bunch of rocks and puts them on this chicken wire table and sprays them out. He takes some more, and does another color. The rocks are pink, blue, yellow, and this nice deep sea-green. Looks like we live at Willy Wonka's factory.

"You can sleep nights," I say. "That blind cow's dead."

"No shit?"

"No shit," I say.

He gets up on his elbows. "Somebody finally hit it? Wandering out on the road."

Sean tells him the story. Money looks sad.

"What's wrong?" I say. "You hated it. Thought you'd be glad."

"Didn't know it was a fucking pet. It had a name," he says. "That changes things." He points across the road. Toller is out by his barn, digging something. "That farmer John?"

"That's him."

"I thought cows were milk and meat and sneakers," Money says. "Didn't know you could have a pet cow."

"Looks that way," I say.

"And the man shot it? Don't they have vets out here?"

"See?" I say to Sean. "Not a stupid question."

Sean explains the details. "He loved her," she says. "He had to be the one that did it."

Money leans back in the chair and closes his eyes. "Glad he don't love me."

➥59

WE GO 3-2 on the homestand, still without Darnell. He's got the OK from the doctor to start practicing with the team tomorrow. He's been doing light work on the exercise bike on his own, trying to stay in game shape. Mobile, the first team we played on the homestand, was in last place and yesterday they picked up Rich Clark in the Galveston dispersal draft. To make room on their roster, they cut Steve Gates, who was once the third-rated shooting guard in the country coming out of high school eight years ago. A hundred schools wanted him—pro scouts drooled over him at the Nike camps. It must seem like a hundred years ago to him now. Gates probably saw it coming—he knew he was done when we traded him. I read it again in the agate type in the transactions section: Mobile (GCL) signed Rich Clark (F) for the remainder of the season. Waived Steve Gates (G). I look at it, thinking, there it is, the end of a career and wonder where Gates is and what he's thinking.

I look at the standings. We're 12-8, with an outside shot at the championship round if we can make up a little ground. The season, though, got shortened from 28 to 26 games when Galveston folded and we need, I figure, at least four of the last six to finish second.

60

I KEEP MY EYE on Keller during our scrimmage. I called Chucky and a couple of other scouts and word is he's staying in the minors. Too small and no shot. His quickness, which is his whole game, isn't much of a factor in the NBA. All the one guards are quick—half of them quicker than Lewie and all of them have better shots. He's a lifer and I figure he'll be happy if I offer him a job to stay with me. He'll get to stay in Sarasota—move to a better neighborhood. His kids can stay in the same school for two years, which has yet to happen in their lives. He cuts down the middle and kicks back out to Money spotted up. Money drains the J.

I watch, thinking about the possibilities for my team—the next team. If I start with Keller, I can build the team around quickness and passing. It can be my team—my players, built around my system. Darnell gets a rebound and kicks out to Hedda, who drops the ball to Lewie in the middle. He runs the break to perfection—hits Hedda on the wing, but she misses a bunny, and there's no trailer. Darnell stayed at the defensive end—didn't even bother to follow the play. The second team gets the board and starts up the floor. I blow the whistle and drop my clipboard.

"Darnell. What the fuck was that?" I walk out on the court. "Follow the play."

He makes this face like he's sorry, but doesn't argue. I wonder what I should do—I pamper him and it doesn't seem to help, I yell and he disappears on me. I blow the whistle and get off the court. "Run the set offense. No transition. We're fine in transition—I want to see the half court."

They go up and down a few times. Money's game is at a plateau. There's no one here good enough to practice with him, and he's falling into some bad habits that'll hurt him at the next level.

"Move left, Kenny. Keep it left. This is practice."

He calls to me as he runs up court, "You tell my man I'm going left, how the hell am I going to get by him?"

"You've told everyone you've ever played you were going right," I say. "Players have two hands."

He gives me a dirty look. A few plays later, he cuts into the passing lane and takes it up court. He and Darnell run a two-man game on one side. The ball goes into the post, our second team doubles Darnell from the weak side. Hedda's wide open under the hoop.

"Cutter," I scream. "See the fucking cutter."

By the time Darnell does what he should, the defense reacts and covers Hedda.

I stop play.

"What was that?"

"I'm rusty," Darnell says.

"If you were rusty, that'd be fine," I say. "You're not trying and you're not thinking. See the open man."

"Woman," Money says.

Hedda raises her hand like I've taken attendance.

I look at Darnell. "Play the game."

We go for another ten minutes. In a half court set, we run a high screen and roll with Darnell and Lewie. Before his injury, this was our second best play—our number one option if Money was cold. Lewie draws the double and kicks back to Darnell, whose got a clear lane to the hoop. Instead of driving, he lets go of a weak set shot—doesn't even leave his feet—that clangs short. The ball drops five feet in front of him—if he'd bothered to follow the shot, he'd have a dunk—but he makes no move to it, and Childs cuts in and takes the rebound. I blow the whistle.

"Drive the fucking ball. The lane was open. Drive."

"Ease up, coach," Hedda says. "D hasn't played in three weeks."

"Are you telling me how to coach?" I say. She's right—there's no sense in yelling at Darnell. I feel like I used to when Linda and I still fought—when we cared enough to fight. I get into a fight, the minute I raise my voice I hate myself, and I want it over. I think, this isn't me, this is my father and I shrink.

Hedda holds her hands up like she's being held at gun point. "Not telling you how to coach."

I always think I'm wrong when I'm in a fight. The thing is, I'm right here—Darnell's dogging it, and that has nothing to do with not playing in three weeks—but I still feel wrong. I look down. "That's it," I say. "Hit the showers."

I pull Hedda aside. "Sorry I snapped. That wasn't about you."

"Didn't think it was," she says.

61

I GET BACK to The Palms. It looks more and more colorful all the time. The rocks shine under the sun, the chairs are pink and orange and yellow, the pool water's clean and clear. It looks edible; like candy. I hear some hammering out back and follow the noise. Bone's behind his work shed.

"Hey."

He's fastening a new joint on a saw horse. "What's up, Ben?"

"The place looks great."

"Some color to an otherwise drab existence," he says. "I've just started. This place is going to be something."

"What?"

"It hit me that day we talked about all your players being stars once and I said it must suck for them here. Then I realized it sucked for me, too. This place needs to be better. Got me off my ass." He stands up, does that cracking of his neck. "A big piece of work. Making The Palms a sculpture. A place of peace."

I look down at the ground. Behind the shed is some Harrington lap cement, some roll roofing, western fiberglass, arrow T-50 staples, and an empty can of Blue Diamond honey roasted almonds. "Lot of work."

Bone takes a drink of water from a one liter bottle. "Not work. I'm a lucky, man, Ben. I can afford to care for this place."

"Thought you hated Parcell's money," I say.

"Never said I hated his money. Said I hated him."

"Isn't that the same?"

He leans back against the saw horse. "He's changed since he bought your team. There's something human about him—the way he talks about you. I'm not so sure about him." He holds the water out to me. I shake my head. "Earl, I still hate. My mother married a loser. Uncle Chicken, though, I don't know. He's started treating me like a person—lets me have the run of the place."

"Still calls you Bernard."

"Bernard is between us, OK?"

"No problem," I say. I drop to the ground and lean against one of the rolls of roofing. "So what's next with the place?"

"A sweat lodge."

"Those sauna things?"

"Native American sweat hole," he says. "A spiritual place. I was thinking stone—but glass brick has been presenting itself to me, lately."

"Presenting itself?"

"That's what things do. Stone wasn't presenting itself. Glass brick was. Things present themselves and you watch and listen." He takes a drink. "You're not a spiritual man, are you?"

"I don't think so," I say.

Bone looks out over the field, squints in the sun. "You're good, though. You've got a goodness. It's rubbed off on Uncle Chicken."

"Please."

"I'm serious," he says. "You should like yourself."

"You don't know the whole picture," I say. "But it's nice of you to say that."

He looks toward the pool. "You like it here?"

"More and more," I say.

He points at me with his bottle hand, then makes one of those someday-all-of-this-will-be-yours gestures. "A place of peace."

62

MONEY AND HEDDA knock on my door. They're dressed in sweats—Hedda's got a ball under her arm, Money holds his keys and wallet in one hand.

"Got an idea for some cash," Money says. "You in?"

"I need more than that."

"Pick-up games," Hedda says.

"The way I got it figured," Money says. "The three of us hit some night courts at Tampa. Get some 3-on-3's for a couple bucks a point."

"Do they know you there?" I say. "No one'll play you for money."

"No one knows anyone up there. It's untapped. I show up with a woman and a old white man in a knee brace, ain't nobody going to be afraid."

"We'll get a nice dinner on the way home," Hedda says.

"Thing is, you got to wear the full brace," Money says. "You got to look bad. Can't be wearing the half brace."

I look at Hedda. She's dressed the part—she wears frumpy sweats that hide an athlete's cut body. She's got make-up on—not a lot, but I've never seen her wear any. She doesn't look like a player.

The full brace—I wore it the second time at practice—runs from mid calf to mid-thigh and has metal supports up and down the sides. It's hinged at the knee and it makes me run like I have a prosthetic. The metal hinges slice into the good leg when I run—it looks like I took a razor to the side of the left leg.

"You've thought this out?"

He smiles. "C'mon. Easy money."

63

WE HIT THE COURTS and play a little H-O-R-S-E, a game of twenty-one. Money's doing a nice job of looking average—he hits less than half of his open jumpers. He still looks like a player—just not a pro. Hedda does a fair impression of a playground player. I lumber around with the full brace, unable to bend all the way, and dribble the ball off my foot a couple of times. It's sad—I look worse than the two of them, and I'm not acting. I walk over to Money.

"Nice job. Just don't screw up your shot permanently."

"Shooting it like Lewie," he says.

"Good idea," Hedda says.

"That's your teammate," I say.

"No offense, coach," she says. "I love Lewie, but he couldn't drop a ball into the ocean off a pier."

Money shows off his bad form. "When you release, you cross hands, and hold the arm. No follow-through." He throws up a brick. The ball has no arc and no rotation.

"You got it," I say. "That's Lewie's shot."

There are twelve courts under the lights. Adult league games are just about over and we should get a few pick-ups soon. We head to the benches and watch the players. Money's sizing them up.

"Big guy in yellow. Can't put it on the floor."

I watch. The courts are beautiful. I love night courts. Asphalt with faded paint in the lane and the three line. Bugs swirls beneath the lights. It's a real playground court—the backboards are metal and the nets are chains. The ball has that clink and bounce instead of a swish when you nail a jumper. Chain nets cradle the ball.

"Little guy in black," Hedda says. "Quick."

"No shot," Money says.

The games finish and we end up picking a game with three guys from the adult league. Two lanky guys and a little guy around five-ten. We go winners to eleven and they touch the ball maybe four or five times. We win, without trying, 11-1.

"Game," Money says as he hits a bank from about ten feet.

I walk over to him. "Your plan isn't working."

"I can only look so bad," he says. "We need a higher quality of beef."

We get it. We play a straight game of winners with three guys who were waiting along with us for the league games to end. We play win-by-two, and the first game goes 18-16 to them. Kenny suggests another game and brings up the bet.

"Buck a point?" he says. "Plus ten bucks a player for winners."

They have one real player—he and Money started to go at it in the first game. I'm not so worried, though, because Hedda can take her man and I'm about even with mine. The real player says, "Two a point. Games to 15. Best two of three. Twenty a player for winners."

We split the first two games. The third game, they're up 8-4 when Money puts on a jump-shooting exhibition. He's in a zone and Hedda and I just give him the ball and hit the boards in case he misses. At 13-8, he finally misses, and I time my jump perfectly. The ball comes hard off the back of the rim and, clunky knee brace and all, I get up for it. I was a shooter and a scorer, but rebounding was always my favorite. There's a satisfaction to the rebound that doesn't exist in the rest of the game. I tip it home.

"Game point," Money says. He tosses in to Hedda on the left wing. She turns and backs her man into the paint. I cut to the foul line and my man doubles down on her. She kicks it out to me, and both defenders run out at me. The other guy face-guards Money—there's no way they're going to give him another shot. I pump fake—two guys fly by me—and hit Hedda cutting to the hole. She hits it, and we win.

"Game," Money says. He heads to the big guy, whose nickname, or name—I'm not sure which—is Rock. "First two games are a wash. We take this by five, plus twenty. Thirty bucks apiece."

"Quick math," Rock says. He looks menacing and I think we might be in for trouble. "One more game."

Money shakes his head. "Got to get home. Long drive."

Rock nods slowly and doesn't take his eyes off Money. He takes out his wallet and gives him a hundred.

"Get you change," Money says and starts to walk to the car.

Rock grabs him. "Keep it. You've played your last game here." He looks at me and Hedda. "The girl and the cripple, too. This ain't a hustler's court."

"It ain't hustling when you win, is that it?" Money says. He gets up in Rock's chest.

Rock steps back. "Go away." He looks at a couple of big guys to his left and holds his hand up. "I'm being very generous here."

I grab Money and limp back to the car with him and Hedda.

"Told you," he says from the back seat. "Easy money."

"Didn't look like it was going to be so easy," I say.

"It's his court," Money says. "He wasn't going to do anything. He's pissing on trees in front of the other dogs. Just saving face."

"How do you know that?" Hedda says.

"Not the first chump I took on his own court. I know how they act." He drops the hundred on the seat between us. "Pretty, ain't it?"

"That court's spent for you," Hedda says. "You played it out for 33 dollars."

"No matter. Not coming back here. Me and Florida, we're parting ways."

64

WE CAN'T DECIDE on where to eat on the way home. We go to a Mexican place that uses lard, and an Italian place that's too crowded. We get off the highway; we get back on. We pass by billboards for strip clubs with 10 cent cups of coffee and Big Daddy Don Garlits' drag racing museum. After a bunch of starts and stops, we end up in Sarasota. We get Chinese take-out and eat it out by the pool at The Palms. Money and Hedda split a six pack of Bass, and I get a two-liter Diet Coke. Bone's put in Malibu lights by the pool. It's a warm night, and both of their faces glimmer from the pool light.

"You play in Europe, coach?" Hedda says.

I shake my head and eat with chopsticks out of the box. The Diet Coke's between my legs I can feel the condensation on my legs. "USBL and CBA."

"Italy," Money says.

"I'm worried about food," she says. "They eat a lot of meat in Europe."

"Where you going to play?" Money says.

"Looks like Spain," she says.

He nods. "Spain's good. How's the league?"

She shrugs. "Women's ball is pretty big there. I'll go for a year, see if I can come back and make the national team."

"Olympics?" I say.

"Now that they let pros play," she says.

I swat my arm trying to get a fly. It gets away. I try to catch it and miss.

"Slowing down, coach," Money says.

"Slowed down," I say. "I couldn't move tonight. Didn't have to fake I was a bad player. I am one."

Neither of them responds. I've brought up aging, losing a step, and that's not something they want or need to think about. I'm that reminder of the guy that didn't make it. Like it or not, I'm the poster child for the run of bad luck—the career that got away.

"Where you plan on being next year?" I say to Money.

He curls his lower lip; looks like he hasn't considered it until I asked. "Don't matter. Want to go somewhere where there's a slot." He puts his box of food down and wipes his mouth. "But where don't matter to me. Vancouver, Toronto, New Jersey, Atlanta. Anywhere I'm wanted."

We sit in the heat around the pool for a while and Bone pulls up in his pickup. He comes to the pool.

"Place looks great, Mr. Fix-it," Money says.

"Thanks," he says. He looks at me. "I got a deal on glass brick. The sweat lodge is underway."

"Good for you," I say.

"Can I get some help unloading the truck tomorrow?"

"We got a flight tomorrow night. Away game."

He shakes his head. "I'm talking morning."

"Morning's cool," I say. "Give me a knock around nine."

He thanks me and leaves. The three of us stay out by the pool past one. The quiet of the night is interrupted only by the occasional sound of Bone working in his shed.

65

THE CORONER ESTIMATES that Darnell Latimore hanged himself sometime between nine and midnight last night. He can't tell for sure, but that's what he thinks—between nine and midnight. Which means, I think over and over, I was out by the pool relaxing and eating Chinese food while he killed himself in his room less than a hundred feet away.

66

THIS IS WHAT I know: Bone knocked on my door at nine and asked me to give him some help unloading his truck. We had coffee down by the pool and decided that if we got some help, the job would take less than half an hour.

I knocked on Darnell's door a few times and got no answer. I started to get worried—I hadn't seen him since I leaned on him at practice and my first thought was he'd taken off or screwed-up and fallen off the wagon. The door was unlocked and I opened it and he's hanging from a ceiling beam, head to one side, his face all swollen and pale, his tongue hanging out to the side like deli meat. A table is knocked over underneath him toward the TV.

"Fuck," I said.

Bone came in behind me. He didn't say anything, just grabbed my arm.

"Call somebody," I said.

Darnell's still in his gym clothes—blue shorts and a gray T-shirt that reads "Property of the Los Angeles Lakers." He's ace bandaged his legs, ankle to thigh so that he looks, hanging above me, like he's in a catcher's stance. His arms dangle at his side. I touch his arm—it's a cold and lifeless as a kitchen counter—and pull away.

After that, it's a blur. I closed the door and threw up over the railing. Stood there for a few minutes. Bone comes back up and tells me he's called 911.

"What'd they say?"

He looks queasy.

"What?" I say.

"They said to make sure he's dead."

I close my eyes and rub my temples. "He is. What else?"

"Don't touch anything and stay put," he says. He leans over the balcony next to me. "They'll be here in a few minutes."

❧67

EVERYONE'S OUT BY THE POOL and the world is a mess. The cops come, and then the coroner. They put that yellow police tape all along the balcony and around Darnell's door. A cop named Carson comes down.

"Who found the body?"

I raise my hand. He asks me to come back up to the room with them.

We get there, and Darnell's still hanging from the ceiling.

"This is the way the room looked when you got here?"

I nod and he scribbles something on a clipboard.

There's another uniform cop in the room along with the coroner.

"What's with the legs?" the cop says.

The coroner, who looks like Ernest Borgnine, looks up and down. "Height," he says. "Too tall to hang himself in this room."

The cop shakes his head and chuckles. "That's a new one."

"This isn't some fucking joke," I say. "Can you get him down?"

Carson grabs my shoulder and leads me to the door. "I'm sorry, sir. I know this is difficult, but I need some information. OK?"

"OK."

He gets the stats he needs. I'm like a zombie, telling him Darnell Latimore, 28 years-old, I don't know the next of kin, call Parcell Industries for more information.

"When was the last time you saw the deceased?" Carson says.

"Yesterday afternoon," I say. "At practice." I think, but don't say, at practice, when I screamed at him. I feel sick and empty.

Two more people squeeze by us and enter the room with a stretcher.

"Can I go?" I say.

"Sure," Carson says. "I'm sorry, Mr. Thompson." I hear this beep and look inside. The coroner jumps, startled, away from Darnell's body.

"Watch alarm," he says and shakes his head.

They stand there with Darnell still hanging, his alarm beeping until the cop goes over and shuts it off.

"Let's get him down," the corner says.

I get to the pool. The team's gathered around, some sitting, some standing. Bone's down there.

"What now?" Hedda says.

"I don't know," I say. "Not a clue."

A couple of minutes later, they come out of the room with the body. Darnell's wrapped in white clingy plastic from head to toe. His legs, I guess they couldn't straighten them. He's lying on the stretcher with his legs tucked up and it looks like he died reading in bed.

I go up to my room and throw up some more until it's just dry heaves. I curl up on the bed and close my eyes. I call Sean, but she's not there and I get her machine. I leave a jumbled message about Darnell and ask her to call me when she gets in.

68

I GO DOWNSTAIRS. Everyone's still around the pool. No one seems to know what to do.

"Someone's got to get Lewie here. And we need to take a vote," I say.

Money looks up. "What's to vote?"

"Whether or not to forfeit tonight's game," I say.

"I can't even think about that," Hedda says.

"Don't seem that important," Childs says.

"Let me call Lewie," I say. "Think about it. We'll vote when he gets here."

I go up to my room and tell Lewie what happened. He's silent for a minute, then says he'll come over. He's about ten minutes away, and I stay in my room. It's hard to think clearly—once I got beaten so bad in a bar fight that I pissed red for a week. My head was sluggish and hurt whenever I tried to think and my eyes wouldn't focus. I'm feeling that, or close to it, now.

When I hear Lewie's car, I head downstairs.

The vote's 6-3 in favor of a forfeit. Hedda, Money and Lewie want to play—which makes sense since they're the only ones that this league or team matter to anymore.

"OK," I say. "I make the call and tell them we won't be there."

"That's bullshit," Money says. "I'm sorry about D—probably sorrier than the rest of you—but fuck him if he's going to cost me."

"This isn't about you," Grant says.

"It sure as hell is," Money says. "We got a game on the schedule, and there's people coming to watch that game. If there's no game, there's no scouts. That makes it about me." He points up at Darnell's room. "I liked D, but he cost himself a shot. He ain't costing me."

"You are one selfish motherfucker," Grant says.

"Fuck you," Money says and pushes Grant in the chest.

"Stop," I yell. "Calm down." I look at Money. "Kenny's right. We've got a game and we'll play it."

"What about the vote?" Childs says.

I take a breath. "This isn't a democracy. I changed my mind. It doesn't do us any good to stay here." I look around. "What are we going to do? Maybe a game would help, I don't know."

Bone comes out of his room. "Called Rube," he says. "He wants you to call him ASAP."

I look at my watch. It's only 10:30 and I feel like I've been up for days.

69

THE GAME DOESN'T HELP, but it does get us out of town for the night. Only Money has any focus—he lights up for 37 on 14-20 from the floor. He was in a zone like nothing had happened and I don't know whether to be envious or disgusted.

Lewie turned the ball over seven times. Childs and Grant said they were playing under protest, and they played like it. We lost 110-91 and, for the first time in my life, I didn't care. The plane ride home was as close to silent as it gets. People made eating noises, read, watched a Seinfeld episode on video, but no one talked much. We got back early in the morning. Hedda asks me if she can catch a ride home with me, instead of taking the van.

We're about halfway home and commuter traffic's heavy on 441 south.

"You OK?" she says.

"Not really."

"I'm not too good with death," she says.

"Who is?"

I stop at a traffic light.

"I'm thinking of leaving," she says. "I've got a contract lined up. I proved I could play here."

"Don't," I say.

"I don't see the point. I feel sick. It's just ugly now. I could use a couple of weeks to get my head straight."

I grip the wheel hard. The car behind me beeps and I see the light's changed. I slide the car into gear. "I could use a couple weeks off, too. I don't blame you. But stay. Please."

She looks straight ahead. "I'll think about it."

"It's only five more games," I say. "Don't walk now."

70

HEDDA AND I go to Terry's instead of The Palms. Terry's at the bar with Sean. We come down the stairs and there's a lot of hugs and I'm sorry's.

"How you holding up?" Terry says.

"Not too well," I say. "Falling apart, I think."

He goes behind the bar and gets us some coffee. "You figure out what made him do that?" Terry says.

"No," I say.

"Sorry I didn't pick up," Sean says. "Your call threw me."

"You were home?" I say, wondering why she couldn't have answered.

"I couldn't talk," she says.

"Couldn't talk?" I say, raising my voice.

"No note?" Terry says.

"No note," I say. "Told me last week he didn't like basketball—never liked it. I didn't believe him." I shake my head. "I should have handled him differently."

"My dad killed himself," Sean says. "I couldn't take your call."

I feel bad for raising my voice, and take a deep breath. "When?"

"Long time ago," she says. "You'll go nuts thinking you had anything to do with it, Ben."

She's right, at least I think she is, but none of it makes any sense. It's like, every two or three minutes, I realize all over again that Darnell's dead. It hits me like news every time.

"At first I was pissed at Money for saying what he said yesterday," Hedda says. "But he was right. D fucked things up for us. He should have done it somewhere else." She takes a drink. "I know that sounds selfish, but it's true."

"I don't think he was thinking about us," I say.

"He wasted everything. If I had his body, I'd be in the Hall of Fame. He blew it and we're all sitting around feeling sorry for him." She raises her glass in a toast. "Fuck you, Darnell Latimore."

"I've got to go," Sean says to me.

"You OK?" I say.

"I'm OK," she says, but she looks frazzled. "Call me this afternoon?"

"I'm in Tampa till five," I say. "Meeting with Parcell."

"Call after," she says and heads up the stairs.

I look at my watch. "I'm going to try for some sleep."

"Good luck," Terry says.

"Coach?" Hedda says. "Does it matter if I stay?"

"It does. To me."

71

"BEN THOMPSON, you look terrible." Parcell motions for me to take a seat.

He's behind his desk and he doesn't seem too upset. He's not happy, but he's the first person I've seen in the past two days that's acting normal. He lights a cigar and leans back in his chair.

"I've got a tip on a player," he says.

"What?"

"Tucker Weatherspoon. Small forward. Right here in Florida. Supposed to go to some big-time school, but he hasn't got the grades. Doesn't want to go Prop 40 or 48 or whatever the hell it is. He's enrolled in some Junior College, but he doesn't have the grades to play, so he's going pro." He smiles. "I've heard good things—great talent, never been coached—and his agent wants us to get first crack at him. He can start now, or you can wait until we're in the CBA. If he's as good as they say, I want him."

"I can't think about this now," I say.

"You'd better. Now is when he's available, and now is when you've got a roster slot. You'd better think about it now."

"I'm dealing with some shit, OK? Latimore offed himself, remember?"

He puffs on his cigar and looks a little sad. "I remember. Don't suggest for a moment I don't recognize that fact, or that I don't care."

"I wasn't," I say.

"You were." He leans forward. "I like you, Ben Thompson. I care and I know this hurts you."

"I feel responsible," I say. I look at the room, the plush carpet with the vacuum tracks all lined up and I feel this heavy sickness.

"You are responsible."

"What?"

"You say you feel responsible, and then you act surprised when I agree? All your friends will tell you that you had no control over this, that it didn't matter what you did or did not do." He points at me. "You should have cut him. You knew it and I knew it. You shirked your responsibility to that young man. I shirked mine when I didn't force you. Don't come in this door, waiting for me to tell you your decisions have no bearing on things. They do. That's what makes them decisions, Ben Thompson—they matter."

"You're saying if I'd cut him, he'd be alive?"

Parcell's face looks drawn and weary. "I'm saying we'll never know, but you did give him false hope." He goes over to the bar to mix a drink. "You want me to tell you it's not your fault? I can't do that. It is, partially. It's partially mine, too."

"You don't seem too broken up about it."

"Do not—ever—tell me how I feel." He takes a deep breath—it's the closest I've seen him come to losing his cool.

"Sorry," I say.

He hands me a bottle of water, and sits behind his desk. "Don't worry about it. This is a hard time." He turns his smoke-sucking ashtray on. "But life, like it or not, does go on. And young Mr. Weatherspoon can't wait until your mourning period is over to select a career path."

"Whose word do you have about him?"

"A few scouts, but I want your opinion. He's got some summer league all-star game next week in Miami. You'll go?"

"How old is he?"

"Eighteen. Just out of high school."

I shake my head. "Too young. Too much pressure for a kid. He should go to junior college."

"Yes, I agree, Ben Thompson. We should have world peace, too. Weatherspoon should get an education and become wise and poised and mature." He holds his hands out. "But he's not going to. That's his decision. He's going to play in the CBA or Europe."

"It's not a good move," I say.

"That's not up to you. What are you worried about, Ben Thompson?"

"Another Latimore."

He winces.

"Hey, you asked," I say. "That's what I'm worried about. I don't want to be part of that."

"Well you are. You were part of it. It's over and done with."

I sit there for a minute.

"Did it ever occur to you that he might be another Kenny Cash, Ben Thompson? Why must you always, always focus on the negative?"

"Guy hangs himself—it's a pretty easy negative to focus on," I say.

"Kenny Cash had a college coach, a USBL coach, and two Italian league coaches. None—not a single fucking one—of them got him invited to NBA camps. You did."

"I don't want to argue, " I say. "I'll look at the kid."

"Good. If he's a real player, sign him on the spot."

"No way to tell from one game, " I say.

"Go back and look some more. When you decide, sign him."

He leads me to the door and puts his hand on my shoulder. "I've had people take care of the arrangements with Latimore's family. Didn't want you to have to deal with it." He leads me to the elevator. "I am sorry, Ben."

"Me too."

72

I TELL TERRY about my meeting with Parcell. The bar is dark and he's got CNN playing with the sound muted.

"You'll look at the kid?"

"We've got four days off around his all-star game," I say. "I've got the time."

Terry cringes a little. "Summer league all-star game's no place to check out talent. Too much showtime, not enough ball."

"I may go, I may not," I say. "He's too young—should be in college—and if he was as good as advertised, he'd skip the CBA."

"Twenty years ago, maybe thirty, I would have agreed with you. But there ain't no difference between college and the pros now. He'll be paid wherever he goes, and he won't learn anything but basketball wherever he goes." Terry plunges a couple of glasses into the washing sink. "He might as well take the money."

"You think so?"

"Hate to say it, but I do."

I look up at the TV. I don't know the topic, but it's one of those call-in shows. Monty from Topeka voicing his opinion on something. The host looks like Dinah Shore.

I shake my head. "The kid may be something. 6'7" and only 180. His body hasn't caught up to itself yet. Could be a player."

Terry frowns. "You're keeping Keller?"

"Yeah. Going with quickness. Weatherspoon's supposed to be quick."

"Check him out."

"And if he's great, so what? I had the best player—the best—I ever saw, and I couldn't get him where he should have been."

"Latimore did what he did to himself. And he had no right to do it—not to you, not to the team."

"You told me so, right?"

He shakes his head. "Not happy about being right."

I look up at the TV. George Kennedy is selling something. Breath mints, I think.

"Darnell's game—back in Chicago, not here—was so beautiful." I take a sip of coffee. "I'll never see another player like him."

"That's where you're wrong," Terry says. "You're a good coach, and I think you should stick with it. But know this going in—you're going to see Darnell Latimores for the rest of your life."

"Bullshit," I say.

"They may not end up dead—it'll be quieter. Washing dishes, hanging around playgrounds and street corners telling everybody how good they were. But you'll see it—huge, disgusting wastes of talent— all the time. It might be next week with Weatherspoon, it might be next month, but you'll see it again and again."

I take a sip of my coffee and don't say anything.

"Not trying to scare you, Bomber. But if you're in it as a career, you've got to get used to great talent that won't pan out. And when you think they won't—know they won't—pan out, you've got to cut the cord."

"You think?"

"I know."

73

SEAN AND I are in bed watching TV. Not much is on, so we settle for "The Good, the Bad, and the Ugly" on TNT. We make fun of it, she calls Clint Eastwood Squint Eastwood, mimics all the tough-guy posturing. It's long, longer than I remember, and when it's over, the meat dehydrator infomercial comes on.

"Can we stay at my place tomorrow?" she says.

I've never seen her place, so I take this as a good sign. "I'm in Miami, tomorrow," I say. "Scouting."

"Right," she says. "Next time, then?"

"You OK?"

"My dad left a note," she says. She's been a little off-balance since Darnell's suicide, but I figured it was none of my business unless she brought it up.

"You don't have to talk about it."

"It's not a problem," she says. "This just brought it back." She rolls a cigarette.

"Can I have one of those?"

"You don't smoke."

"I used to. I miss bad habits."

She rolls me one. I light it, and it's amazing—it tastes as good as the last one I had five years ago.

"'Dissonance,'" she says.

"What?"

"My dad's note. Dissonance. He was a musician—prodigy, boy genius, the whole bit. He had perfect pitch—a lot of people claim that—but he had it. He used to quiz me when I was a kid. A car horn would beep in traffic and he'd say 'what note?'" She takes a drag of her cigarette.

"He could tell?"

"Trick question," she says. "All car horns are in A or F#. But he could tell jackhammers, people's voices when they talked, anything. Everything was notes to him."

"And?"

She shrugs. "And he went nuts. He sat me down when I was ten, maybe eleven and he told me to picture a note as an inch. Perfection was the center of the inch. If everyone were in tune, they would all be at the center of the inch. But he said there was no center. That's what his ear led him to—nothing was ever in tune—everything in the world rattled against him."

"How long did this go on?" I say.

"A year, before he killed himself. It got ugly. He sound-proofed his studio. If you talked, he'd put his hands over his ears and shriek. He couldn't handle sounds." She takes a drink of water. "Everything became noise."

"Sounds awful."

"It was," she says. "Words, voices, hurt the most. When people talked, he just screamed and ran away." She looks at the TV. "He shot himself."

The guy on the TV is turning a hunk of wet meat into jerky. The sound is off, but I've seen it before, and I know he's going on about the outrageous prices they charge for store-bought jerky and how that's a thing of the past with your new dehydrator.

"I'm sorry," I say.

"Don't be," she says. "I thought you should know. I'm not right, Ben—I flip out and can't sleep sometimes and all I want to do is shut off my brain. I have dreams where I smash my head against a wall until I'm dead."

"That's what I miss about drinking," I say.

"What?"

"Being able to shut off my head. Everything else is cool—I don't miss drinking the way I used to. But some nights, I can't slow down. Can't stop."

"Do you think you'd kill yourself?"

"Not so much anymore," I say. I picture Darnell, hanging from that ceiling and wonder what he was thinking, wonder how bad and empty he had to get before that made sense. "Sometimes." I lean over to her. "Are you OK?"

"No," she says. "Sometimes I am and sometimes I'm not. Can you handle that?"

"What?"

"Me. I'm giving you an out here. I know you're having a hard time—I'm kind of high-maintenance."

"Who isn't?" I say. I finish my cigarette. "I don't want an out." She puts her head on my chest. "You want to come to Miami?"

"No," she says. "I've got to work, and then I promised Bone I'd help out with his sweat thing."

"You're sure? You can come."

"We don't have to go everywhere together," she says. "That's not what I meant—I need a lot of space. I just wanted to warn you—if I go through a hard time, don't take it personally. If my problem's with you, I let you know."

"Fair enough," I say. I tend to take things personally and wonder of this is going to work. I feel uneasy, but I don't say anything.

She flips the sound back on the TV. She needs the sound on to fall asleep, so the set stays on. I'm watching old government films of duck-and-cover drills on the Discovery Channel when she falls asleep.

74

WE BEAT BATON ROUGE and Mobile at home—close games, but Money's finishing with a flourish. He hit for 32 against Baton Rouge, and then had an unstoppable game against Mobile. He put on one of the greatest jump-shooting shows I've ever seen. I yanked him mid-fourth with 51. A league record. A shitty little league, with no history, but 51 is a night in any league. Scouts from New Jersey were at both games and he's got the official invite—in four weeks, he's in Jersey's rookie camp.

I fly to Miami to check out Weatherspoon. Before the game, I'm watching him run some shooting drills and Jake Stuart—my old agent—comes up to me courtside.

"Ben. Back in the game I hear," he says.

I shake his hand. "Back in the game."

"Who you looking at?"

"No one specific," I say.

He smiles. "Bullshit. Weatherspoon's mine," he says. "I'm the one that got Parcell to get you down here."

"Why the secrecy?"

"We didn't have the best parting of the ways," he says. "I wanted to apologize, but I wanted to make sure you were here first."

"No hard feelings," I say. "I was washed up."

"You didn't want to hear it," Jake says.

I remember me calling his office, screaming at his secretary, calling him every name in the book. "I know."

"So, we've got a clean slate? You won't squeeze my client over something between us?"

"There's nothing between us," I say. "History." I take a seat. "Tell me about him."

"He can play," he says. "Cocky, but a good cocky. Good kid. Good family. Can swing between the two and three spot. Slasher. Can get to the rim on anybody. Dr. J ability." He points out to the court at Weatherspoon. "A blue chip."

"He's so perfect, why are you talking to me and not Jerry West?"

"His body's not ready for the big-time."

"The body? That's it?" I say. "What about the grades?"

"He's sharp. Not a dumb kid."

"Coachable?"

"He is. A little bit of a floater—too good for his own good. Needs someone to focus him."

I watch him shooting 15 footers. Nice rotation; decent form. The horn sounds and the teams head to the bench.

"I'll look," I say. "If he's got anything, I want to meet him."

"You're our first choice, Ben."

Mid-first quarter, Weatherspoon starts to take over. He gets to the rim well—has a fearless drive. He's all grace and no power, but that could be fixed with time and a weight room. His dribble's too high—he's a forward, not a two guard. His legs are great—he can jump out of the gym, and his lateral quickness is awesome. On his first step, he's got a minor foot hitch—when he's going to drive, he pulls one foot back before he pushes off. That won't hurt him in the CBA, but it'll kill him in the big leagues. He plays a kind of defense that's rare in such a raw player.

"Well?" Jake says at half-time.

"We've got first look?"

He holds his hand up in the scout's-honor pose. "You do."

"I've got three days off before our next game. I'd like to get him up for a scrimmage before I lose Cash. This week, or next—whatever works. See what he does with a real hand in his face."

Jake frowns. "He won't travel without his parents."

"Fine," I say. "I want to talk to them, too. Call Parcell. Let's get him up and have a look." I get up.

"You're taking off?"

"I've seen enough," I say. "Let's see some more up in Sarasota. Too big a fish in too small a pond here."

"Moby Dick in an ice cube tray," Jake says. "This kid's special."

I hold up my hand. "I'll see him next week."

75

I GET BACK from Miami and the sweat lodge's about halfway done—the glass brick shines like diamonds in the sun. Hedda, Bone and Sean, sit in the middle of the circle of glass, passing around a bottle of wine. All of them are naked from the waist up. Sean's wearing cutoff jeans and cowboy boots. Bone's in his cutoff Chino's and Hedda's got a pair of boxers and nothing else on.

"Am I interrupting?" I say.

Bone is on his back with his eyes closed. "You got a gutter mind, Ben," he says. "We're communing."

I look at Sean. "A place of peace?"

"It is," she says.

"Hey, coach," Hedda says. "What's the word?"

I look at her and look away. I feel awkward seeing her naked. "The word is you and Money just became the old folks on the team."

She looks sad. "Lewie's gone?"

I forgot Lewie was the oldest with Darnell gone. "No. Didn't mean to scare you. Lewie's still here. But I think we're signing some 18 year-old."

"Eighteen?" Hedda says.

"Just turned," I say.

"Eighteen," she says and whistles. "So when do we see this boy wonder?"

"A few days. Maybe next week," I say. I look around. "Place looks good."

Bone looks up at me. "Getting there."

Sean pokes Bone in the side, takes the bottle from him and drinks. "Ask him," she says.

"Ask me what?"

"You want your navel pieced?"

"Hadn't thought about it," I say. "This been a topic of conversation?"

"My idea," Sean says. "Bone found a cleansing stone and set it in a hoop."

"A cleansing stone?"

"Your aura," Bone says. "Cleanses your aura."

"Please," I say. "My aura's fine—just had it checked."

"What could it hurt?" Sean says.

"Me," I say. "It could hurt me."

Hedda stands up and points to her mid-section. In her navel is a silver hoop with a black ball. "Got mine."

"If you jump off a bridge, do I follow you?"

"It's quick—not much pain," Bone says.

Sean takes a sip of wine and passes the bottle to Hedda. "I'd think it was sexy," she says. She lights a cigarette and sits with her legs wide apart, her elbows on her knees.

"How sexy?"

"Worth-your-while sexy."

I look around at the candy cane Bone has turned The Palms into. The deck chairs, and all their colors. He's got two neon palm trees—about six feet tall each—by the entrance. It's gaudy and beautiful in an odd way.

"What the hell?" I say. "I suppose my aura could use a little cleansing."

It's over in less than fifteen minutes. We do it on the ground inside the sweat lodge. Bone wipes my navel down with this yellow/orange fluid that I think is iodine. He sticks a hollow point needle—it's not that big, a lot smaller than the ones they use to drain water off the knee—up through the belly button, and slides a silver hoop through. It stings, but it's not too bad. The ring is almost a full circle, and the stone fits in the space in the ring and is held there, I guess, by tension. Sean takes pictures the whole time—when I wince as the needle pulls through the skin, she says, "That'll be a good one."

Bone holds a mirror to my torso. "What do you think?"

I feel a little silly. "I'm too old for this."

"You're younger than Rodman," Hedda says. "And he's full of piercings."

"He's still playing—when a millionaire does it, he's quirky. I do it, I'm just dumb."

"It's hot," Sean says.

"Talk like that could change my mind."

"Be careful with it," Bone says. "It's all muscle—the risk of infection is bigger than with the nipple or the genitals."

"Really?" I say.

"Muscle rejects," Sean says.

Bone gives me a little tube. "Put this on it every few hours, and keep it clean."

Money pulls up on his bike and comes over, a basketball under his arm. He looks at all off us half-naked in a dirt pit surrounded by glass walls.

"Do I want to know?" he says.

Hedda points to her stomach. "Bone's doing them for free. You want one?"

Money shakes his head and laughs. "Fuck, no." He turns around and walks toward the pool. "Another day in Freakville," he says.

76

SEAN HAS TO WORK late so I stay home alone. I think of going down to Terry's—Money's trying to organize a nine-ball tournament—but I'm tired, my stomach's hurt and swollen from the piercing, and I sit in bed with the TV on and the sound off. Every few seconds the neon palm trees light up and hum—the room flicks green and dark, green and dark. Behind my drapes, I see the bugs smashing themselves against my porch light. Some make a noise when they hit the glass.

I rub my stomach and it's warm to the touch. A crazy thing to do—I'm not sure why I let Bone do it, other than that I feel at home here. I take a deep breath and start thinking back—where I was a year ago tonight, two years ago tonight, and so on. I get to six years ago Linda and I were married and falling apart in South Miami.

I rummage through my wallet for Linda's number—she's remarried and living somewhere in California. It's not too late there, so I call.

"Linda?" I say. "It's Ben."

There is a pause. "Are you in trouble?"

"No," I say. "The opposite, I think. I'm OK."

"Then why are you calling?"

"Because I'm all right. Things are working out," I say. "I'm a coach—a CBA coach. I got my navel pierced today."

"That's," she says and breathes hard into the phone. "That's good for you. You're happy?"

"Overall, I think I might be," I say. "One of my players killed himself." I look at the TV and Andy Griffith is giving Opie some fatherly advice out on the porch. "Darnell Latimore. Do you remember him? He and I played at Chicago in '84."

"That's a long time ago, Ben. I try not to remember anything." She doesn't say anything for a moment, and I know the look I'm getting. I've seen this look, she's got the phone cradled on her shoulder and her arms crossed—I'd bet my life on it. "Another lifetime. Why, really, are you calling me?"

This isn't going the way I'd planned. I wanted some closure, some we-had-some-good-times, some good-lucks. "To tell you everything was OK—I'm not a total fuck-up anymore—and to see how you were. I didn't mean to bother you."

"You are no longer capable of bothering me." I hear her breathing and some motion and clanging—it sounds like she's in a kitchen. "I'm fine. And I'm glad, honestly, that you're OK. But I don't know you and you don't know me. We are not part of each other's lives. Take care of yourself, Ben. Be happy. But leave me out of it."

She hangs up.

I hold the phone after she hangs up. There's the click, a few second's pause, and then the dial tone. I put the phone down, light one of the half-cigarettes Sean left in the ashtray and stare at the ceiling fan. Linda stops talking when there's nothing left to talk about. Me? I'll talk shit to death, getting nowhere the whole time. I should never have called. The room's quiet again, and I hear the buzz and hum of the neon palm trees.

⚾77

FOR SOME REASON I wake up real early—the sun's not up yet—and I'm wide awake. I flip through the early morning news shows, but they're depressing as all hell—shootings, murder stats, the whole bit—so I make some coffee and head down to the pool. I sit in one of the yellow recliners and wait for the sun to come up. There's noise coming from Bone's work shed. I walk over and knock.

"You're up early," I say to Bone.

He's welding something. He shuts off the flame, and lifts his eye shield. "Up late," he says. "Haven't been to bed."

"Really?"

"I'm full of energy. I've got nothing but plans for this place." He stands up and walks to the door, pointing to the abandoned half of The Palms. "After the sweat lodge, that's next. Blowing out the walls— turning it into three apartments."

"No more small rooms?"

"On this side, I'll keep them small—maybe double them and make them art lofts."

The sun begins to peak up behind Toller's farm. "Sounds good."

"You can have one of the big rooms," Bone says. "If you want to stay."

"That's cool?"

"I'd like it if you stayed."

The new team's going to up in Tampa, and it'd be more logical to live there. I think about Sean, about the way she said we're not married, when I got upset at her, and wonder what I should do. She and I might work; we might not, but if I move to Tampa, we're probably done. "I'd like to stay here," I say. "I can help out. I can still hold a brush."

"You going to have much free time?"

I think about it. More traveling, more games, more players. "No," I say. "Not a lot."

We decide to have some coffee out by the pool while Bone shows me his plans for the place. I get the coffee and he meets me at the pool with a banana box.

"What's up?" I say.

"A gift," Bone says. "Sorry about the wrapping."

"A gift?" I say and open the top of the box. Inside is a small scale basketball court—the floor is hardwood, the rims are black metal with little glass backboards. The detail is great—he's painted in little three-point line and lanes. At center court are two figures on crucifixes. Down by the time-line, it's signed The Two Thieves: Glass, wood, and metal. Bone. On the other side of the little court, the whole team has signed their names, with the exception of Money, who always uses the dollar sign on his autographs. "Thanks. It's great."

"Do you get it?" he says.

"I didn't know it was something to get," I say. "I'm a little dumb about art."

"No," he says. "That's a good impulse. Most of my stuff works against meaning, but this one's a message for you. You know the two thieves?"

"No."

"Dismas and Gestas. They were crucified along with Christ," he says. "Think about it. Christ up on the cross. Dismas asks what he's there for and Christ says I'm dying for your sins. And Dismas and Gestas say, our sins? Everyone's sins, Christ says." Bone takes a sip of his coffee. "So Dismas and Gestas are thinking: If he's dying for my sins, what am I dying for?" Bone stands up. "So, even if you buy the whole Christ dying for our sins, son of god bit—which I don't—you have to see that even he let a few slip through the cracks."

"I'm still unclear on the message."

"The message is some of us go south on our own—no one to blame, no one to take the rap," he says. "You can beat yourself up forever about what happened here." He points up to Darnell's room, which still has strips of yellow police tape around the door, flapping in the wind. "Or you can move on."

"You got the dimensions perfect."

"Hedda helped me out there," he says and sits in the candy apple red recliner. "I'm sorry if it's preachy—I don't usually work with a message. In general, I hate them."

"No," I say. "It's great. I love the way it looks." I look down at the ground. "I'm touched."

"Everyone was worried about the way you were taking it, Ben." He points at the side of the floor with all the signatures. "People care about you."

And I'm thinking back to my first meeting with Parcell and him making me say people love Ben Thompson. I think about Linda and Leon Garriss, and a bunch of others and think and people hate Ben Thompson.

I'm still unsure of which category I fall into.

"You OK?" Bone says.

"Yeah," I say. "I'm good. Thanks."

"How's your navel?" he says. "Any infection?"

"No," I say. "Hurts a lot, though."

"It's a cleansing pain."

"Really?"

"Maybe, maybe not," Bone says. "Just trying to put a good spin on it for you."

I look at his chest. He's wearing a blue checked flannel shirt, but it's not buttoned and you can see the nipple rings and the navel hoop. "The pain doesn't bother you?"

"I like it," he says. "It's a high. My cock bled a lot, though."

"You have a ring in your dick?"

"Ring and a post," he says. "You want to see?"

"That's a little personal, no?"

"Don't go prude on me, Ben."

"OK," I say. "Whatever."

He pulls his shorts up and pulls his dick down his thigh. He's got a little hoop through the slit in the penis, and a rod behind the head. It looks kind of nice, but I hope it's not something that turns Sean on. "Bled a lot there," he says, pointing to the hoop. He pull his shorts back down over his leg.

"Didn't that hurt? I mean really hurt?"

"The hoop did. The post, I got it done right by some voodoo woman in New Orleans. Very spiritual," he says. "I had spontaneous orgasms for two days afterwards."

"No shit?"

"I stopped counting at twenty-five. Couldn't sleep. Couldn't leave the house, for obvious reasons."

"You're pulling my leg."

"I'm not. The body does strange things."

"I guess," I say. Some birds chase each other in circles above the buildings. "What does Hedda think of those?"

He shrugs. "She seems to like them." He finishes his coffee and puts the mug on the ground.

"You going to miss her?"

"She's got to do what she does. And Spain's the place for it," he says. He looks sad. "But, yeah, I'll miss her."

78

TUCKER WEATHERSPOON and his parents come up to Sarasota. His folks are up in Tampa at some posh hotel that Parcell owns. Before practice, I walk over to Money.

"I'm putting you on the second team," I say. "Putting the kid at the two, and I want you to work him."

"How much?"

"Work him."

"Don't give him anything easy, work him, or send him crying into his momma's arms, work him?"

"Let him play," I say. "But make it hard."

I blow the whistle and the scrimmage starts. It's a little harder on Weatherspoon than it was in Miami, but not a lot. He works Money well on defense, and holds his own on offense. He gets a couple of good picks and absolutely explodes to the hole. He's shy of his jumper—if I'm going to have him and Lewie together, I'm going to have to find someone with a jumper to take the pressure off them.

We go all out for half-an-hour and I tell them to hit the showers. I pull Money aside.

"What do you think?" I say.

"He can play. He's no me, but he can play." Money mimics Tucker's high dribble. "You know I could have picked that any time I wanted?"

"I know," I say. "Puts his head down when he drives. Did you catch the hitch?"

"That'll hurt him," Money says. "Used to getting to the rim too easy."

"So what do you think?"

"You're asking my opinion?"

"I am."

We're by the corner—out of bounds about five feet behind the three line. Money launches a jumper that hits nothing but net. "I'd say you've done better," he says smiling. "But, with me gone, he might be your best bet."

I shake his hand. "You are gone."

"I am, and no offense, but as long as you're minor league, I don't want to see your face unless again unless you got tickets."

"No offense taken. I want tickets, though. You come down and play Orlando or Miami, I want to watch."

He motions to the locker room. "You going to sign the kid?"

"I think so."

He looks out at the practice court. "He could do worse," he says, which is as close to a thank you as Money gets, I think. He thanks people the way golfers hit those dinky little two inch putts—like it takes all the effort in the world and they shouldn't have to bother with it.

"Thanks," I say.

Money walks out onto the court and starts his shooting drills.

79

I CALL PARCELL after practice and give him the go-ahead on the paperwork. We talk a little about details, and he asks me to come up later in the afternoon.

I'm the last one in Parcell's office. Jake's there with Tucker and his parents. Parcell is behind his desk. He welcomes me into the office, tells me to grab whatever I want to drink.

I shake Jake's hand, and he introduces me to the parents.

"So, where are we?" Jake says.

Parcell leans forward, and addresses Mrs. Weatherspoon. "I've talked this over with Coach Thompson, and we're prepared to offer Tucker $25,000 for the season."

"Way too low," Jake says.

Parcell smiles, but it's a condescending smile. "I was not talking to you, Mr. Stuart. Nor was I finished." He looks back at Mrs. Weatherspoon. "$25,000 for signing. If he will agree to certain incentive clauses, the figure could be bumped up considerably."

"What are the clauses?" Jake says.

Parcell looks at him, and then back to the parents. "The $25,000 is guaranteed. If Tucker agrees to have a tutor—at our expense—and get his test scores up to college standards, we're prepared to add another $15,000."

"I like that," his mother says.

Parcell points to me. "Thank Ben Thompson. We both feel it's important that you get your degree," he says to Tucker.

"I understand, sir," Tucker says.

Parcell wave the sir away. "Call me Rube, son."

And I'm thinking, I don't get to call him Rube.

"What else?" Jake says.

"A signing bonus if he agrees to the terms. And a bump if he gets called up."

"You'll pay him more if he gets the call?" Jake says. "Makes no sense."

I lean my chair toward Jake. "It's important that this is a stepping stone. No one—including us—wants Tucker to be a career CBA player."

We go over more details and I begin to get bored with the money talk and the insurance talk. It seems over and Parcell turns to me.

"Anything to add, Ben Thompson?"

I look at Tucker. He really is a kid—bone-thin, his suit hangs from him like a scarecrow. He's trying to grow a beard, but his hair is all patchy. "You can play. But you have a ton of bad habits. That's not your fault. If you don't listen to me, though, it is. My job is to make you the player you can be. I'm not promising you anything except a spot on the team. I'm not even promising you'll start. You'll get a chance to play pro ball, and I'll work you harder than you've ever worked." The kid nods after every sentence. "I need to know you want this. I'm not going to invest my time in someone who doesn't work."

"I'll work," he says.

I shake his hand, and then his parents. "As far as I'm concerned, you can start now—with this team—or wait a few weeks and start fresh in the CBA. Whenever you're ready, you're on my team."

Tucker smiles. "There's a game tomorrow, right?"

"There is," I say. "And I could use you. I'm down to eight players."

Mr. Weatherspoon shifts in his chair and looks at me. "You had a player commit suicide," he says.

"Yes," I say.

Tucker shakes his head, and Jake looks upset. Mr. Weatherspoon looks at both of them. "I need to know this," he says. He looks back at me. "What happened?"

"I'm still not sure," I say.

Parcell says, "Darnell Latimore was a drug addict. He'd probably started using drugs again. There was nothing we could do."

I look at Parcell and want to punch him. But it wouldn't solve anything, and I begin to realize that's how people are going to talk about Darnell from now on, if and when his name comes up. And ten, twenty years down the road, I'll probably still be wondering if I could have changed any of it. "We don't know if he was on drugs," I say and look at Parcell. "I don't know what happened, Mr. Weatherspoon."

He sits back in his chair and looks satisfied with my answer. "I had to ask," he says.

"Of course you did," Parcell says.

Jake leans forward. "There are still a few things we need to work out." Jake and Parcell start haggling over little details again, and I excuse myself, say my good-byes, and take off for home.

80

SEAN AND I STAY at her place—which is brighter than my place, and has more books than I've ever seen in an apartment— and lounge around most of the day. I've missed this—doing nothing with someone you're comfortable with. Around three, she tells me she's got writing to do and she'll see me tonight for dinner. I drive to Terry's. My car's driver side door has stopped opening, so I have to crawl in through the passenger side. By the time I get the car started, I'm drenched in sweat.

It's ninety out, and probably less than seventy at The Bunker. Terry's behind the bar, eating a sandwich and reading the paper.

"Called you last night," he says.

"Wasn't home."

"With Sean?"

"I was. We're going to dinner out on the bay tonight. Watch the pelicans and the dolphins."

"Good for you," he says and gives me a cup of coffee. "What's the news?"

"I'm staying put," I say. "Bone and I talked about it. Staying at The Palms for the season."

"Glad to hear it. It's been good," he says. "Having you here."

"Same here," I say. "You've helped a lot."

He shakes his head.

"Listen," I say. "I know we've talked about this, but I want you to reconsider about the job."

"Please, Bomber."

"I've got a real team. I need another pair of eyes. I need a scout and a coach. You're perfect."

"I am not," he says. "Man who doesn't want the job is not perfect for the job."

I take a sip of coffee. "Listen to me." I look at him. "Will you listen to me?"

"You're not listening to me."

"Parcell and I are on the same page. I took the Weatherspoon kid, and he's got clauses in the contract for education, for incentives. Parcell did it my way."

"For now," Terry says. "Young man pops a tendon, you call and tell me how nice your boss is."

"You said I'd see another Latimore, and I did. This kid's special."

"Being special don't make him special. You don't know what it'll take to keep him on track."

"Maybe not," I say. "That's why I could use you."

"The minute you lean too hard on him—for his good—you know who's going to be talking to him?" He counts on his fingers. "His agent, his family, his girlfriend, and every single hanger-on in his little world." He leans forward. "And all of them will be telling a young, impressionable man, that you're wrong, he's right, and that you're just out to get him. The worst thing you can do to an eighteen year-old is give him a ton of money and tell him he's always right. That's what you're up against." He stands back and shakes his head. "You can't do it, anymore. You can't coach when the player is worth more than the coach."

"He seems like a good kid," I say.

"He might be," Terry says. "Now. Good luck keeping him that way when he starts hitting for thirty every night. When he starts beating up on CBA retreads and you tell him his game still needs work— see how responsive he is then."

"Stop," I say. "You're depressing me."

"Don't mean to."

"My fault," I say. "I brought it up." I finish my coffee. "Will you come tomorrow? Last game."

"For this team."

"Right," I say. "For this team. You should see this kid—he's something to watch."

"Like who?" Terry says and smiles, talking in EV talk.

"Great slasher," I say. "Big problems in his game, but he gets to the hoop like Bernard King."

"King?"

"Not his whole game, but the way he drives."

He wipes a glass dry and hangs it on the rack above his head. "You're not trying to rope me into the job?"

"I'm not. I want you to see him play."

"I'll come. But I won't take the job, Bomber. I'm done."

"I understand," I say and get up from my stool.

"You don't understand," he says. "And I hope you never do."

❧81

W E'VE GOT CLOSE to a full house—which surprises me since we're out of competition for the championship round. Parcell sits behind the bench with the Weatherspoons. He's got his program wound up in a tube like Wooden, and he winks when I come out to the court. The team runs warm-ups. Parcell leans forward and motions me over to him.

"You will dress better when we're CBA, won't you, Ben Thompson?"

"Probably not, " I say. I lean closer to him. "You sure you want Tucker's folks this close to the bench?"

"What's the problem?"

"I swear a lot," I say. "And I'll probably swear at their kid before the night's over."

He taps me on the head with his program. "Didn't use disappearing ink on the contract, Ben Thompson. His parents are no longer important." He turns and gives them a smile and a wave. "They're meaningless to us, now."

I look at him. He was acting like their best friend at the meeting, and I worry a little about staying useful to Rube Parcell. "Right," I say.

"Do your job, Ben Thompson. Don't question my judgment."

I turn and watch the team. We've got the Bayou Dogs in town, and we should kill them—they're in last place since Galveston folded, and we've swept them so far. Money looks loose—he's headed to a pro camp, and he's strutting around the court like he owns it. Across the way, Terry, Bone and Sean sit together about midway up the bleachers. I give a wave, mostly to Terry since I wasn't sure he'd show, and they wave back.

The horn blows and the team comes to the bench.

"This is it," I say. "Let's have some fun with it."

From the start, Lewie blows by their point, breaks down the interior defense, and we've got open looks all over the floor. Money opens 4-for-6, Hedda has a couple of put-backs, and by the time the Dogs call time, we're up 18-5. The team sits on the bench and I raise my hands. "Nothing to say. Keep it up."

Late in the first, we're up 29-13 and Money steps in the passing lane and picks one off on the right wing. He takes off for the hoop, and Rudy Larson, their shooting guard, cuts off his path. Money steps on Larson's foot and turns his ankle, and drops to the floor, rolling around. He screams.

I look at him rolling on the floor, thinking it's over. I can't move and I feel sick. I'm watching him, thinking injury, rehab. He stops rolling and I finally get over to him.

"Don't move," I say.

He waves off my help. "Let me up. Just turned it. I'm OK."

"Stay down," I say.

He gets up on his feet and limps for two steps and starts to hop to the bench. He winces as he sits down.

"You sure you're OK?"

"Hurts," he says. "But it's just a sprain."

"You're done for the night."

He looks up at me. "I can play."

I lean down close to him so the other players can't hear me. "You will not fuck yourself up in a nothing league. This league is over for you. I'm not risking it."

He looks like he's about to argue, but he stops. "I hear you, coach."

"Weatherspoon, you're in for Money."

Tucker springs off the bench.

I put my arm around his shoulder. "Nervous?"

"Little," he says.

"Just play. Same game—basket's the same height. Don't try to take over. Get in the flow of the game."

"OK, coach." He runs out on the floor. I pull Lewie aside and tell him to try to get Weatherspoon some looks.

I sit back on the bench next to Money.

"You scared the hell out of me," I say. Sprains can hang around, make you favor a leg. Money's going to need all the breaks he can get to make a roster and I never should have put him in a position to get hurt.

"I'm fine."

"I didn't know that."

"Neither did I. At first."

"Ice it down," I say. "Take care of it."

They make a little run and the game stays mildly competitive into the second. Weatherspoon's playing a little tentative—he's passing off when he has a lane, he jab-steps when he should drive. I call a time-out.

"Where's the guy I saw in Miami?" I yell at him. I act more disappointed than I am.

"Sorry, coach."

"Drive the fucking ball, Tucker."

"Right."

"Your man better than you? Can he stay with you?" He shakes his head. "Then take him off the dribble. He's a chump."

I send the team back out and sit down.

"Jumping ugly at the kid," Money says.

"We'll see if it works."

Two possessions later, Weatherspoon takes his man off the dribble. No hesitation, no jab-step—he just explodes by him and dunks baseline.

"Yes," I scream. "That's it, Tucker."

We start to pull away and Weatherspoon starts tearing up the gym. Near half-time, they try their third defender on him. At first, it was all penetration, but he's got the rhythm, and he starts hitting short jumpers. He takes the ball on the left wing, cuts middle, and spins back with a pretty turnaround from about fifteen feet out.

"He might be something," Money says.

"He might," I say. And I think of all the things that could go wrong and all the ways I could screw up.

Hedda grabs a rebound and kicks it out to Lewie, who hits Weatherspoon. Tucker takes the ball off the right wing and goes underneath for a reverse dunk.

Money claps and kicks his feet out. "He's almost as much fun as me." He pokes me in the side. "Your kid's feeling it."

Everything Tucker throws up is falling. You have nights like this where you just can't miss. The Bayou Dogs don't have anyone with his quickness. Not all his nights will be like this—he's too thin and too young and he's got bad habits and he will struggle—but tonight, he's got it going and he can't be stopped. It's an amazing feeling—it's like luck, but bigger—like every coin on the planet fell heads-up in your path and they're all yours. The crowd loves him, and he's in that zone you play for—live for. I look at him and think Darnell had this—this and more—and it wasn't enough.

Two minutes before half-time, we're up 61-39 and Tucker takes his man off the dribble and pulls up and hits from about ten feet off glass. He runs up the court, smiling. He might be a player—his lateral quickness and his first step, even with the hitch, are something you don't see much.

"I'm done for the night?" Money says.

"You are."

"Guess I'll just relax and enjoy," he says. He grabs one of my bottles of water and takes a drink.

Money leans back and crosses his legs, full of confidence. I look at him, hoping everything falls into place and this really is his last night in the minors.

The next time we have the ball, Weatherspoon gets it on the left wing and he has that look in his eyes that says to his man, I can't miss. I won't miss. Do whatever you want, try whatever you can, but it doesn't matter—you don't exist. It's just me, the ball, and the rim and the sun might burn out and the world might stop turning before I miss again.

About the Author

ROB ROBERGE is the author of the book of stories, *Working Backwards From The Worst Moment Of My Life* (Red Hen, 2010) and the novel, *More Than They Could Chew* (Perennial, Dark Alley/Harper Collins, 2005). He teaches writing at the Antioch University Los Angeles, MFA in Creative Writing, UC-Riverside's Palm Desert MFA program and the UCLA Extension Writers' Program, where he received the Outstanding Instructor Award in Creative Writing in 2003. His stories have been featured in *ZYZZYVA, Chelsea, Other Voices, Alaska Quarterly Review* and the "Ten Writers Worth Knowing" Issue of *The Literary Review*. His work has also been anthologized in *Another City* (City Lights, 2001), *It's All Good* (Manic D Press, 2004) *SANTI: Lives of the Modern Saints* (Black Arrow Press, 2007) and *Orange County Noir* (Akaschic Books, 2010).New work has appeared in *Penthouse* and *Black Clock, 11*. He plays guitar and sings with several LA bands, including, among others, the punk pioneers, The Urinals. In his spare time, he restores and rebuilds vintage amplifiers and quack medical devices. www.robroberge.com